TUDOR COURT

Books by K. N. Proctor

Questions for the Possibilities (non-fiction, 2007)

The Other World (2020)

TUDOR COURT

K. N. Proctor

Punctuation uses British style

Cover illustration: Hannah Wood

Copyright © 2022 K. N. Proctor

No part of this publication may be reproduced in whole or in part, or transmitted in any form, or by any means, electronic, mechanical, photocopying, recording, or otherwise, nor in any form of binding or cover other than in which it is published without the publisher's prior written permission. For information regarding permission write to
proctorkn@protonmail.com.

ISBN 978-1-7357469-3-7

Printed in the United States of America

'... true good lies not in the esteem of men but is hidden in a pure conscience and that those are not truly men who, clinging to things destined to perish, do not recognise their own good.'

Hugh of St Victor
c. 1096 – 1141 A.D.

CONTENTS

CHAPTER ONE

TUDOR COURT

'For time is like a fashionable host
That slightly shakes his parting guest by the hand,
And with his arms outstretched, as he would fly,
Grasps in the comer: welcome ever smiles,
And farewell goes out sighing. O, let not virtue seek
Remuneration for the thing it was;
For beauty, wit,
High birth, vigour of bone, desert in service,
Love, friendship, charity, are subjects all
To envious and calumniating Time.'

William Shakespeare
Troilus and Cressida

Tudor Court stands alone at the end of a pebbled drive in the Northumbrian countryside bordering the English county of Cumbria. The road leading to Tudor Court is off two side roads and would be found by few without prior knowledge. Its owner delights in this privacy, prefering to invite her guests. For Elizabeth Fennington enjoys her own company too much to lend it out randomly.

Surrounded by four hundred and fifty acres of rolling English countryside that include a hearty stream, a lake, and long established rambling English gardens, Tudor Court is a beautiful representation of the old traditional English estate. A variety of wild flowers, thick and thriving, light the meadows in a profusion of colour. Screened from the road one trusts that by taking the lightly gravelled drive from the end of the cul-de-sac address one will arrive at the house. A four minute drive on the private road leads to a bend which partially reveals the ancient stone chimneys of the house. In moments, there amongst the trees, Tudor Court presents herself, stately, beautiful, with the charm of centuries imbedded in her ancient oolitic limestone.

The original house was built on the same grounds in the 1500's. The name derives from these origins and the original tenant, an illegitimate branch of King Henry VIII. Tudor Court, deeply set amongst ancient pine, beech, and oak trees, is an innate part of its landscape. When first seen in full from the entrance to the pebbled drive she presents a grand and gentle edifice which speaks of history and earthly permanence. Three imposing peaked rooves catch the eye, and the seven stately stone chimneys standing in position at the front, sides, and back of the house are as sentries at the gate. Atop the middle peak is a significant rose window and as one approaches the house a large bas relief of the Tudor rose echoes the past. Set low, to the right side of the main entrance the white and yellow of the rose have long disappeared. The four stems of green have been naturally replaced where moss has been allowed to grow. The red remains. Ivy grows up the sides and not the facade of the house and wild flowers, encouraged to grow near the entrances, provide lively colour. A simple wrought iron gate at the side opens to the expansive, ancient, well tended gardens.

The stone of the structure, butter smooth to the touch, holds a barely detectable yellow tinge. Perhaps because such stone is unimaginably older than man those who inhabit its walls live in a world prime for imagination. This may be something of the enchantment of Tudor Court and here is found something of her character. Surrounded by expansive parkland, backed by woods, and with heather moorland beyond the woods Tudor Court has about her an unexpected sense of the wild. Yet like her name, Tudor Court is an historic expression of English civilisation.

The house was restored in the early 1800's. In the care of the Bedford's, Tudor Court's owners at the time of the major restoration, an historic house became a warm welcoming home, open to guests, filled with light, and with its original character remaining unscathed. Rooms speak of the classic, of something learned over the ages and retained. While Tudor Court was built on a smaller scale than the major manor houses of its time, and as such is most suitable for the current owner, nothing was stinted in the size of the rooms nor the height of the ceilings. The stairways are simpler, more practical than those of the great manor houses. The windows in particular speak of a grand house made for living. A few of the windows were opened and lengthened further in the Georgian period to be waist height to within inches of the thirteen foot ceilings. While most of the windows are still sashed, Elizabeth's uncle had placed full open panes in the bedroom Elizabeth chose and in her bathroom, as well as in the smaller drawing room, and the library.

Elizabeth's grandparents purchased Tudor Court and from her early childhood Elizabeth had loved the house and especially the grounds. One summer she asked her grandfather if she could visit for a week to explore the grounds and ride her horse in the meadows and along the forest paths. Her grandfather, assuming Elizabeth had asked her parents, gave his consent. When she arrived with her horse in tow and without her parents a lengthy phone conversation ensued between her grandfather and her father. In the end Elizabeth was allowed to stay. Every summer the tradition had endured until Tudor Court became Elizabeth's own upon inheriting it from her childless uncle.

Elizabeth lived happily at Tudor Court and as happiness found is often better shared Elizabeth made the decision after a year of quietly enjoying the seasons to share Tudor Court's beauty. This decision led to inviting guests to regular gatherings; soirées, dinners, teas and luncheons, garden and tennis parties, eleven months a year.

Elizabeth's invitations are a personal and particular offering to a guest's sensibilities. The handsome example for life Tudor Court mirrors is inspiration to any who would seek a better way to live. The offer is, in a simple way, as the proferring of a new hat, inviting a guest to don a new mantel, inspiring one to a greater worthiness for the day. The inspiration is to the greater meaning to be found in the ancient Greeks' understanding of the value of good, truth, and beauty. Tudor Court reflects this revelation.

CHAPTER TWO

THE CASE OF ANGER

Angus Erhly was angry. He was angry about the increased taxes the Council had relegated to his property. He was angry about his neighbours thinking it better for Britain to stay in the EU, and angry about friends wanting Scotland out of the UK. He was angry that people preferred Elizabeth Fennington's parties at Tudor Court over his parties at Wrathmore House.

Angus's anger might have been funny except that it left him with a permanent scowl and a voice with untoward fire in everything he said. While his anger toward the government's theft of his money and his neighbours idiocy in their political views might well be warranted, he knew that his anger toward Elizabeth Fennington and the success of her parties was not. In fact, he quite liked Elizabeth. But he held it against her that invitees would refuse his invitation for her's. Though he had to admit and he did so, grudgingly, that he enjoyed attending her parties, what he could not fathom was how anyone could think Tudor Court surpassed Wrathmore House and its farm and grounds. He had far more land and more animals. He had more servants, the house itself was larger, newer, though this latter fact may actually have been a negative in the charm department.

Nonetheless there was no getting away from it, Tudor Court out shone his offering every time with respect to where people wanted to be.

Angus recalled with some perturbation his most recent experience at Tudor Court. He had gotten into an argument with one of the other guests over the proper training of one's dog. Angus held that one must establish a personal relationship with one's dog. This required the proper investment of time. Most importantly it meant talking to one's dog. The other fellow thought this ludicrous and argued that the latest trainers knew what they were doing. One must send one's dog with a handler to follow along with other dogs and their masters or handlers. This included obstacle courses to learn obedience. Angus thought this nonsense and a waste of time and money. Most importantly rather than getting one further along with one's dog the dog thought you an idiot for doing those ridiculous obstacles and lost respect for you. The other fellow had laughed and told Angus that dog's don't think. Angus retorted to Brumeyer, 'It is you Brumeyer who does not have a proper thought in your head. I feel sorry for that fine Irish Wolfhound of yours, he deserves a smarter master.' At this point voices were raised in anger. Brumeyer had the discipline to control himself and suggested they cease the argument. They had shaken hands and moved to opposite ends of the room.

Angus apologized briefly to Elizabeth before he left and Elizabeth, gracious as ever replied, 'I enjoyed seeing the sparks fly and it gave more energy to the room.' Angus could not deny that Elizabeth was the gracious hostess. He respected her aplomb, manners, and intelligence. While he didn't understand why she invited the groups of people she did, he appreciated that she offered much opportunity to mingle, connect, and learn true hand the latest news locally and even internationally. He was recognising lately that he was fighting with himself as much as with any outside opponent. He was angry with life, or at least with many aspects of it. Angus wanted to repent. He wanted to relax. Elizabeth was relaxed, particularly comfortable in her own skin. This he thought, is what most makes her so particularly attractive. There had been a time that he'd wanted to stay away from Tudor Court and he had done. As a result he'd lost an opportunity to purchase some land he had long sought. He would have been introduced by Elizabeth to the party in question and with little doubt his overture to purchase would have led there and then to the purchase of the land he wanted. After that disappointment he always accepted Tudor Court invitations.

'Who is playing Fergus?', Angus asked his valet as they decided on his tennis togs for Elizabeth Fennington's afternoon tennis party.

'I understand Sir, Batholomew Atwater is attending', Fergus began.

'Oh yes, Atwater is a great friend of Miss Fennington's. Does he still play tennis?', Angus said with disbelief.

'I understand Mr Atwater is a very good player Sir', Fergus replied.

'Hmm, indeed', Angus said under his breath. 'Who else will be there?'

'Suzanne Abbington-French will be attending', said Fergus.

'Oh yes. I've seen her before at Tudor Court, though not elsewhere', he replied ending in a somewhat snobbish tone.

'Then there is Sir Hamilton Atwater, a distant cousin of Bartholomew Atwater's', Fergus said with a just perceptible element of pride in his knowledge, knowledge he knew would catch his master's attention.

'Oh?', Angus was surprised and fully attentive now. 'I hadn't connected their relationship. Sir Hamilton will be there? Indeed', now a small smile creased the corners of his mouth, imperceptible to most but not to Fergus who knew his master well.

Fergus turned his head and bent down feigning to brush some invisible lint from Angus Erhly's jacket. He too allowed himself a smile, a reward for managing to rowse the same response in his employer.

'Well, this will be a fine afternoon Fergus', Fergus's employer's spirit had sparked up. 'I'll wear my Albert Whyte jacket.'

'Yes Sir', said Fergus and picked up the jacket he had laid out to return it to the closet. 'I'll just be a moment Sir, your Albert Whyte hangs in the adjoining room.'

Angus grunted his acknowledgement and returned to his revery. Well, this should be a fine afternoon, he repeated to himself. Sir Hamilton. His knighthood is of the first order. For a moment Angus's smile was about to be replaced with his usual scowl. This was because his own order of honour was a grade lower than that which allowed for knighthood. However, his next thought helped maintain his temporary cheerful disposition. I wonder what kind of tennis player he is? Now his smile remained firmly in place, for Angus was a very good tennis player indeed.

Fergus returned with the Albert Whyte jacket. The Albert Whyte had been tailored by the finest Saville Row had to offer. Angus had instructed them to weave threads of his family colours into the lapels and they had achieved a solution with a most subtle effect. Only a discerning eye would detect the few strands of red intermingled with the deep green that ran along the edge of the length of the lapels.

'Fergus', Angus stopped for emphasis.

'Yes Sir', came the expected response.

'I will wear my Royal Victorian Order.'

'Yes Sir. Shall I retrieve it now Sir?', Fergus inquired with due reverence in his voice.

'Yes Fergus that will be fine', and a note of graciousness had entered Angus Erhly's voice.

The Royal Victorian Order, third class, was duly pinned to the lapel of the Albert Whyte jacket and now Angus Erhly, well coiffured, standing six feet one inch, with a rare upward crease to his mouth, stepped into his classic 1963 dark green Bentley. He had originally intended to drive himself in his Land Rover however the knowledge that Sir Hamilton would be attending Elizabeth's tennis party ignited his need to display his own position in the world. With his order of honour neatly adorning his jacket, he could hardly swing himself in and out of his Land Rover. And so his driver had given the Bentley a quick buffing and was now driving the few miles on country roads to present Angus Erhly at Tudor Court.

Who the other guests would be hadn't mattered once Angus knew Sir Hamilton would be attending the tennis party. He sat in the back of his Bentley while his driver drove him between his estate and that of Tudor Court. He gave his thoughts over to the afternoon with Sir Hamilton Atwater. As he did a spark of anger arose within. Why could Elizabeth manage to entice Sir Hamilton when he could not? Of course he had never invited Sir Hamilton. An uncomfortable blushing heat arose in his face as he knew he'd never invited anyone of that ilk to Wrathmore House for fear of the invitation being refused. The blush of anger would soon turn to bright red if he continued contemplating this state of things.

'Your forests are looking particularly lush this year Sir', Reginald, his driver, commented. Reginald, noticing the rising colour in Erhly's face, and recognising its source, as all in his household did, made his attempt to diffuse the heat.

'Yes, they are', Angus replied.

The driver's comment moved Angus's mind to the fact that out the window of the Bentley the view was still of his own property. He sighed, and contented himself with the thought, my estate is much larger than Elizabeth's, and, yes, the forest does look very fine indeed.

The party gathered on the outdoor terrace which ran the length of the west side of Tudor Court, with the two tennis courts just below. A cocktail before play helped to keep the company in jovial spirits.

'Friendly tennis, not too competitive', Elizabeth always said.

Angus was seated beside Suzanne Abbington-French. Suzanne was an attractive woman Angus decided. She's tall, he said to himself, without being an amazon. She has fine bone structure, everything in proportion. And, she has quite a lovely face. Her auburn hair tied up for play suits her, showing off her high cheek bones. But it isn't too neatly tied and the strands falling loose give a good English effect Angus thought, not that perfect European look which annoyed him. She has nothing to hide Angus surmised. If she can play she will be a good partner for me he concluded. The other woman who sat across from him and beside Sir Hamilton, he hadn't caught her name, looked decidedly dowdy in comparison. His partner and he would play doubles first against Elizabeth and Batholomew, while Sir Hamilton would play singles with that woman.

The first set proved harder than expected to win. Fergus was right, Barthlomew was a good player. Elizabeth and Suzanne were an even match. Angus pulled himself and his partner through and they won the first set 6-4. Angus could see, having glanced over at the other court a few times, that Sir Hamilton played well but not as well as himself. He would offer Sir Hamilton a singles game after the current final set. The next set was more easily won. Angus, having sized up his partner's play as well as that of their opponents, served and volleyed, coming to the net more frequently. The score was 6-2. Angus was determined to play Sir Hamilton one way or another and if possible manage not to be rude to Suzanne. After two sets, Elizabeth and Bartholomew said they were content and repaired to the terrace leaving the four to decide on sets of singles or a set of doubles.

They played doubles much to Angus's chagrin. However, Angus, a disciplined chap, put it out of his mind determined to win. Angus played the first set of doubles partnering with Sir Hamilton and the second with the other woman, Astrid Markum. The men initially tried not to beat the women too soundly. However Suzanne and Astrid gave it everything they had. The men had to give up their gentle play and press harder in the second half of the first set in order to avoid making a poor show. When they switched partners Angus fought back with stronger serves and quicker shots to Sir Hamilton's side of the court. But Suzanne and Sir Hamilton teamed well at the net and back of court, while Astrid did not like going to the net. Angus was running forward and back and they lost a few games because of it. It went to a tie break. And Angus managed to save the set by acing Suzanne.

At lunch Angus finally had his chance to talk with Sir Hamilton. Elizabeth had seated the two across from each other.

'You have a large estate not far. I understand it practically borders Tudor Court', said Sir Hamilton generously.

Sir Hamilton was much accustomed to people wanting to engage him. He had a simple kind way of allowing them to do so.

'Yes, I'm fortunate to have Elizabeth as a neighbour', Angus managed to reply graciously.

'She is a good neighbour to have. Her father was neighbour to my own father in Monaco when we had a home there.'

'Oh?', Angus was interested.

'Yes. My father loved to sail and there is a lot of good sailing in the Mediterranean. My mother liked to socialize', Sir Hamilton laughed. 'And so they managed well together', he ended with an almost shy smile.

'How well did you know Richard Fennington?', Angus asked, curious to learn the connexion.

'Quite well I'd say. He was lawyer for my first business venture. My father had recommended him. Richard was thorough and most capable of placing things in simple language for his client to easily understand. Have you ever encountered a

New York attorney who shows himself off with an arrogance of knowledge?', Sir Hamilton asked.

'No, I have not had experience with New York law', replied Angus.

'Well, it's an experience to have only if you can laugh while he goes to the bank with your money. I'm sure there are plenty such lawyers in London. Richard was a very different sort. I liked and appreciated him, not only for his knowledge, for his character.'

Angus was listening and looked over at Elizabeth. She and Bartholomew were engaging Astrid and Suzanne in a conversation. But Elizabeth looked up to meet Angus's eyes and smiled. Had she heard the subject of their conversation? He wasn't sure.

'I saw Richard socially on occasion and we became friends over perhaps twenty years. He died a few years ago. He was a man I was happy to have known', Sir Hamilton finished.

Angus thought this quite the recommendation of character and was quieted by it. They both sipped their wine.

Then Angus asked, 'And how did you get to know Elizabeth?'

'We met in Monaco at their home there. The Fenningtons grow up entertaining', he laughed.

Angus noted that Sir Hamilton liked to laugh. And his laugh was a rich laugh, from deep within. It made Angus smile. Angus noticed that too.

'Being brought up with company around, strangers and old friends mixing in, makes you quite comfortable with conversation and noticing of what others need for their comfort. I believe we are reaping the benefit here at Tudor Court', said Sir Hamilton.

'Yes', Angus paused. 'And you are right Elizabeth's guests do seem most comfortable.' He paused again. 'I enjoy myself here', he said slowly, his voice relaxed, lower and quieter, than his usual strong cadence.

'Cousin', Batholomew and Elizabeth had come over to where Angus and Sir Hamilton were seated. 'We have not had a chat in a long time. May I interrupt and ask you for a walk in Elizabeth's garden?', Bartholomew asked his relative. He bowed his head to Angus silently asking to be excused for his interruption.

'Angus will you join me for a walk?', Elizabeth asked. 'Astrid and Suzanne have gone off to the kitchen garden to examine cook's arrangement for the herbs', Elizabeth made her appeal.

'Yes, delighted', Erhly replied with energy, smiling.

'Good, come with me then', and she took Angus's arm and led him out of the dining room, leaving Bartholomew and Sir Hamilton to their walk in another part of the garden.

'The darling buds of May', exclaimed Elizabeth. 'Don't you adore this time of year in the garden?', she asked rhetorically.

Angus had to pause. He registered that in the last hour he had paused quite a few times and that this was not his style.

'Well', he began. 'I don't think I've been in my garden these last two weeks.'

'Why ever not?', Elizabeth questioned, turning to him.

'I've been busy, I guess', he said in a low, somewhat ashamed voice.

'You have missed the first blossoming of the ornamental cherry trees. I believe you have a fine row of pink and white trees not far from the house', she said.

'Yes, yes I do', he acknowledged.

'And what of your lilacs? If you have a good gardener he won't have pruned them all at the same time. And you should have their mauve beauty and lovely fragrance to enjoy', she continued.

Angus was considering Elizabeth's interest in the garden. She had led him out a side door and directly into her garden. As she spoke they passed flowers, bushes, and trees, of which he did not know the names. He felt sure that Elizabeth knew all the names.

As they approached a flowering bush with delicate and fragrant yellow blooms he said, 'This I do not have, what is it?', Angus gestured to the bush.

'Isn't it lovely', Elizabeth exclaimed. 'This is perhaps my favourite bush, genistra, I love its fragrance. Do you?', she asked.

Angus, unaccustomed to sniffing flowers, leaned in hesitantly. Elizabeth stood waiting for his response. He took a long inward breath with his nose close to the flowers. And then he took another few sniffs.

'Yes, I like it very much', he replied contentedly.

Elizabeth smiled, 'I'm glad. It is truly lovely. How are the wisteria this year?', she asked him as they continued deeper into the garden.

'The what?', he responded.

Elizabeth laughed, 'Oh come now, every good Englishman is familiar with wisteria.'

'Wisteria, yes', he realised he did know what that was. 'Well, it looks pretty much as always. It's still hanging from the sides of the house and along the fence that leads from the house toward the forest', he added.

'You must ask into its health of your gardener. He will tell you more. You have an abundance of ancient wisteria. And the lavender colour against the greys of your house and the boards of your fence are a beautiful contrast. You don't want to lose it', she finished.

Angus nodded sheepishly. Then he asked, 'Will you tell me what the flowers and bushes are as we walk?'

Elizabeth beamed, 'I'd be delighted. Do you see ahead off to the left the pink and white cascading bushes? Those are pieris.'

As they approached Angus asked, 'Is that sweet smell their fragrance?'

'Yes', she affirmed. 'If we pause a moment another little breeze will waft more fragrance to us. To appreciate the moment is to grow in appreciation', Elizabeth offered. 'And there it is'.

Elizabeth bubbled over with the laughter and delight of a child. For a little breeze had come from the direction of the bushes straight to them bringing the sweet spring smell of their newly blossomed flowers. Angus smiled at Elizabeth and her joy, and at the vibrancy of life on display.

'I want to show you something', she took his arm again and led him through a narrow entrance in a long hedge. 'There is a place I'll show you a little deeper in just before the woods', she said in something of a covert whisper. 'It is where I go when I want to be truly alone, quiet, and to contemplate', she shared.

They walked a corridor created by the bushes and trees flanking them on either side, Elizabeth leading the way. Two squirrels paused to peer at them from the trees. Angus caught sight of a robin turning its head to observe them and he tingled inside. The hair on my arms is standing up he said to himself as he experienced the intimacy of the moment. They were bending their heads to low hanging ancient beech branches. And there in a small open area was a wood bench seat where the sunshine could come in, as it was now, full strength.

'We can sit here', said Elizabeth, and moving to the bench she sat down. Angus sat down beside her.

'It's as in a museum when you want to take in a great painting. You have to pause and sit. You have to be quiet, stop, in order to try and see what the creator wanted to share and hear what he wants to say to you', she said.

They sat there quietly. Angus, caught up in the moment and with only intermittent recognition of the fact, listening to Elizabeth and sensing Nature in their midst, sat very still. A robin flew to the neighbouring oak tree and onto a branch which extended into this special spot. He sat there looking at them. Angus wondered if this was the same robin who'd turned his head to look at them a few minutes ago. Perhaps he'd followed them. He rested on the oak branch just the right distance to watch them as though not to intrude. A nearby bird began to sing. Angus turned to the sound to see the bird that sang.

'You won't see him', Elizabeth said. 'I only hear that song here. I don't know what bird sings it.' The sunlight lit parts of the trees in front of them, leaving some leaves in shade. The contrast of lit green and dark green was strikingly beautiful. Angus was aware of nature here in a way he had never before been. He took in the striking beauty of sunlit trees and shade, the movement of a new and delicate branch affected by the breeze, the song of the bird, and the divine fragrance of the mock orange tree Elizabeth had introduced. And he recognised the presence of a new knowledge. Angus now knew why Elizabeth exclaimed surprise at his indifference to the wisteria and his insensibility to the scent of flowers, to all the new life of Spring. He had locked himself out of life, of the life around him, of life that now he could see, smell, feel, and hear, of the life calling him. And he felt the last vestiges of anger fall away, slip off his shoulders as a mantel no longer needed because Spring had arrived. As he sat beside Elizabeth he felt himself relax into the truth of the good, great beauty, all around him.

CHAPTER THREE

THE CASE OF ENVY

Evangeline Erstwhyle envied Elizabeth Fennington. Evangeline envied everything about Elizabeth. Elizabeth's face was the cause of men turning their eyes from Evangeline when Elizabeth entered the room. Elizabeth's tall slender figure was in distinct contrast with Evangeline's rather short and decidedly stocky form. And Elizabeth's wealth was far beyond Evangeline's means.

Evangeline had a pretty face. Her eyes were grey not quite blue, and well spaced. Her brow was delicate, a narrow arched line above her eyes. She had a clear complexion and straight white, though small, teeth. Her nose was a little too small. Yet all these features taken together formed a pretty face. In comparison to Elizabeth Fennington, comparisons which Evangeline was ever wont to make, Evangeline was merely pretty and far from the beauty Elizabeth embodied. Elizabeth's bone structure was of that superior sort that represents elegance, a classic referrence to beauty over the ages. The high cheek bones would hold her features firm well into her fifties. She had a fine complexion with good colour. Full brows arching beneath a broad forehead suited her intelligence and strength of character, character apparent to any good observer. This character and intelligence were well reflected in her hazel eyes, eyes that danced with light and delight for life and intention to carpe diem. Her nose, straight and of medium size, reflected the ancient Roman concept of beauty. A strong, yet feminine chin, with a good mouth, not small, not too large, with the unusual trait of the upper lip set slightly further out than the lower lip further distinguished her face. All her features seemed to have been fashioned by the expert artist, created that together the face offered a vision of classic beauty. At five feet eight inches with an exquisite slimness, long of leg with lovely long arms in likewise proportion, Elizabeth glided into a room. Her lustrous brown hair shining with auburn streaks, especially apparent in the summer, perfectly framed a well formed head. Her sincere smile warmed the recipient and invited response and good conversation.

Evangeline contemplated all of Elizabeth's fine features. Then, again, she made the comparison to herself. Evangeline recognised that her face was pretty. She knew the same could not be said for her figure. Her tidy waist she ever endeavoured to accentuate while hiding her stocky legs beneath long skirts. Rather than glide, Evangeline padded along with something of a plodding gait, all grace absent. And while Evangeline was always reminding herself that Elizabeth's face and figure were far superior to her own, she paid little attention to Elizabeth's intelligent and considerate conversation. For if she had, she may have noticed a good insightful mind and a most kind nature.

Then there was Elizabeth's money. Elizabeth's grandfather, Arthur Fennington, had been a wealthy American industrialist. He had also been a wise investor in the markets. Arthur left his fortune to Elizabeth's father, and to his other son, upon his request, he left Tudor Court. Elizabeth's father had taken good care of the fortune. Richard Fennington had not pursued the business, preferring a quieter life in the law. He had invested a good portion of the money, and while not as bold as his father, his prudent investments resulted in most of the money being intact at his death. And he had left it all to his only child, Elizabeth. Tudor Court became Elizabeth's when her uncle died.

Elizabeth was born in London and lived initially in America. Her parents returned to Great Britain and settled south of London when Elizabeth was a young adult. Elizabeth had studied English in Edinburgh. Her family had kept in good touch and in good relations with Elizabeth's grandfather's connexions, and these connexions were long standing and well established. It was these fine relationships Elizabeth now parlayed into great enjoyment for herself and for fruitful lessons for life for those of her guests who would climb in the world.

Elizabeth's expenses were relatively low. Her grandfather had purchased Tudor Court years before for cash. It had been well maintained under the supervision of her grandmother and there were no extraordinary expenses now for its upkeep. There was also a comfortable flat in Monaco overlooking the sea. It too had been paid for by her grandfather who had enjoyed the high life there as a good change from his busy life in America and rural life in England.

Elizabeth had a tidy income through the investments left her by her prudent father and, a small income, through her writing. Her articles; political perspectives (quite conservative), and cultural observations and insights (theatre, art, gallery exhibits) were much sought after by publications both in Great Britain and North America. This offered a steady if modest source of cash while keeping Elizabeth ever articulate. Her personal luxury, and much enjoyed, was for clothes and shoes. An Italian sense of style for clothes that fit and hung to perfection accentuated her figure and thus her overall beauty. Elizabeth's sense of luxury would have extended to book purchases had not her grandfather left a large and exceptional library.

As Evangeline thought of it it was Elizabeth's money that was the greatest object of envy. Nothing could match the power and the freedom possessed as a result of having a lot of money. Nothing could remedy Evageline's sense of powerlessness and feeling of relative enslavement as a result of having only, just enough money. Of course by most standards Evangeline was well off. She had good food to eat, a comely roof over her head, and money to spend reasonably. Yet the nature of envy is to look outside oneself, though not beyond. One looks at one's neighbours to find those greener pastures and finds what one has not and when one does find it, to settle there and build up resentment of another's better fortune rather than appreciate what one has. To be envious is far more satisfying for a certain nature than to be humble and grateful, appreciative of what is. Now if Evangeline had been able, and she may well have been able if she had been interested, to turn her mind from envy to appreciation, she would have increased her happiness substantially.

'Who is at table this evening Mamam?', Morris asked his mistress as the two surveyed the dining table.

'John Hobart, Elliot Newman, Syril Arlington, Evangeline Erstwhyle, Suzanne Abbington French, Alison Martin, and Mr Atwater', Elizabeth responded to her housekeeper, and at the last name Elizabeth smiled.

'I'm glad your friend is able to join you Mamam', Morris smiled in response to his mistress's evident pleasure in contemplating the company of her friend Bartholomew Atwater at dinner.

'You'll seat Bartholomew by me as usual Morris?', Elizabeth asked rhetorically.

'Oh yes Mamam', Morris said, and then paused in hesitation.

'Yes Morris?', Elizabeth asked responding to the hesitancy.

'And . . . where shall I seat Miss Erstwhyle . . . ?'

'As usual, beside one of the gentlemen', Elizabeth said, and having heard an extra note in her housekeeper's voice, looking at him asked, 'What is it Morris?'

'I know it is not my business Mamam, but why do you invite Miss Erstwhyle?'

Elizabeth looked again at her housekeeper, 'Why, what are you thinking?'

'She envy's you Mamam', Morris bluntly stated.

A little smile arose on Elizabeth's face. Then she said, 'Perhaps you've also noticed', and she paused, 'or guessed, that there is something I enjoy even more than writing my articles and reviews. People are fascinating, in particular, character is fascinating. And it is when given opportunity for reflection that people are most rewarding to observe. Because it is, other than in a crisis, in those moments that one most sees character.' She smiled at Morris and gave him a little nod. And with a mischievous appreciatively raised brow, added, 'One may encourage those moments of reflection, one never know's where that opportunity for reflection may lead.'

Evangeline arrived early. When the bell rang at 7:13PM, Chalmers, who was just contemplating the proper positioning of his cravat, frowned.

'I wonder', he said to himself. Then he said, 'Miss Erstwhyle I believe?'

A minute and a half later, in which time the bell had been pressed again, Chalmers opened the door and said aloud, 'Miss Erstwhyle I believe?', with exactly the same intonation he had just used to himself.

Miss Erstwhyle, completely missing his meaning, said, 'Yes. Good evening', as she stepped across the threshold and immediately began to look about her.

'I believe Miss Fennington will be down at 7:30. Would you care to wait in the parlour', Chalmers said, and not as a question.

Evangeline, studying a portrait in the entry hall, took her time in responding.

'May I show you to the parlour?', Chalmers added.

'The parlour. I am enjoying perusing the paintings here', Evangeline said. And as she finished she moved further down the hall and stopped in front of another oil painting.

'Chalmers, was that a bell I heard?', Elizabeth's voice came wafting down to them from above. And then her head appeared from the top of the second floor.

'Oh Evangeline', she said most graciously. 'I'll be down in a moment.'

Evangeline smiled slowly and meaningfully at Chalmers. Chalmers bowed his head ever so slightly and walked away down the hall.

Evangeline, delighted to be alone in the grand entry hall, continued to move about. Next she examined the large portrait of an old Fennington family member, and finding him too sombre moved to the great hearth. As she was about to move further down the hall, Elizabeth came lightly down the staircase.

'Evangeline, how nice to see you again. I'm pleased that you have come', Elizabeth greeted her warmly. Evangeline smiled. Observing Evangeline's progress along the entry hall, Elizabeth asked, 'Would you like a wee tour?'

'Yes, thank you, that would be very nice', came the reply.

Elizabeth walked beside Evangeline down the wide hall further into the house, pointing out a painting on the wall beside them, a rare tapestry hanging nearby, or a vase from another part of the world. Evangeline's thoughts clouded with envy as she accompanied her hostess and experienced the beauty and charm that Elizabeth enjoyed everyday. Elizabeth and Tudor Court suit each other, Evangeline thought, though she did not know that it was character over charm that most distinguished them and made them suit each other so well. Evangeline's thoughts regarding Elizabeth continued to flow. Elizabeth's vibrant energy lights up rooms, so too Tudor Court feels alive with history and charm. There is something, not only of a great charm, she came upon it, of substance, in them of both. For all the fog created by her envy, Evangeline was not an unintelligent woman.

The warmth and light from the open fire in the hearth they had just passed was so inviting that it caused Evangeline to begin to chat. As they stood before a portrait Evangeline said, 'When I was at the Tate the other week I was admiring all the new artists.'

'Oh?', Elizabeth offered.

Evangeline, perhaps expecting a more loquacious response, tried again, 'Are you a great museum goer?'

'I do go to the National Gallery. My favourite museum is the Metropolitan Museum of Art in New York. I don't tend to like modern art', Elizabeth said.

'Oh?', Evangeline, repeating the syllable she had heard a moment before, injected it with a slightly sarcastic tone. She continued in this vein, 'I can appreciate all forms of art, sculpture, painting, crafts.'

There was no reply. Undiscerned by Evangeline, Elizabeth was not a chatter. Elizabeth swept on ahead further into the house pausing in front of a large painting hanging near the entrance to another room.

'This landscape, I've been told, was my great grandmother's favourite place outdoors. She lived not far from this forest and meadow. It's in Derbyshire', Elizabeth offered openly. Evangeline observed in silence.

Elizabeth continued, 'She would let her pony graze as she walked the hills.' Elizabeth smiled and looked to Evangeline who was now gazing up in awe of the beauty of the sunlit landscape in greens and golds. Chalmers appeared in the hall announcing to Elizabeth the arrival of the other guests.

'Thank you Chalmers. Shall we join the others?', Elizabeth asked of Evangeline whose face betrayed a bewilderment at the beauty to which she had just been introduced. It was a bewilderment for the great beauty of the landscape, and the subtle beauty in the story of life when beauty is appreciated.

Chalmers had ushered the others into the drawing room where cocktails were being served. Elizabeth entered the drawing room with a warm smile for all her guests. Chalmers held the door open for Evangeline who trailed behind.

Turning to include Evangeline Elizabeth said, 'I believe you all know one another.' As they had all met before they were welcomed without introduction.

Elizabeth wore a subdued chocolate brown evening length sleeveless gown with matching slipper shoes. Her brown hair shone with its natural tinges of auburn, and with a slight wave flowed down her back. After some minutes of simple conversation she invited her guests to move to the dining room.

'You are seated beside me Bartholomew', Elizabeth said.

'Thank you my dear', her friend replied.

Morris had arranged Evangeline's place at the other end of the table from Elizabeth. Evangeline, approaching the table along with Elizabeth and Bartholomew ahead of the others noticed her name card. She made a quick decision, I will seat myself beside Bartholomew Atwater and hear his and Elizabeth's entire conversation. Suzanne Abbington-French, seeing her name, walked around the table to seat herself beside Bartholomew. As Bartholomew pulled out her chair, Evangeline sat down in it.

'Oh', Suzanne exclaimed softly. Hesitating only a moment, she looked round the table for the empty place that was now hers. Syril Arlington was smiling at her with a slightly raised brow, as he held the chair beside his own for her.

Evangeline contemplated Bartholomew Atwater as she sipped from the crystal water glass. Bartholomew Atwater was a man more than thirty years Elizabeth's senior. A man of medium build who had kept his shape and with his energy undiminished, appeared more youthful than his actual years. He immediately ignited an enlivening conversation with his hostess.

'Your recent review of 'Pirates at Sea' had me laughing so thoroughly that I called for tickets. I brought my niece to see it the other night and we both enjoyed it very much. Given the title I wouldn't have given the play a second thought, assuming it to be a silly comedy about pirates. The script was brilliant. And seeing those City financial johnnies get their knickers in a knot had me laughing almost non-stop.'

Elizabeth laughed, 'Once you know something of what the play is about the title works well.'

'How did you and Elizabeth meet?', Evangeline interjected into the conversation at the pause.

'Goodness', Bartholomew paused, 'We seem to have known each other always. Haven't we my dear?', he said turning to Elizabeth.'It must have been your father who introduced us.'

'It was', Elizabeth exclaimed. 'You had a lovely place in the Lake District. What was it? Oak Walk?'

'Yes', he nodded and smiled in remembrance.'That's been gone more than ten years now.'

'My father gained an invitation for a week one summer', Elizabeth said speaking to Evangeline. She continued, turning back to Batholomew, 'And I guess you didn't object. I have to admit that at the time I liked walking in the forest more than I thought of you', and she laughed.

'Object to your father and his family's company? Certainly not. Your father offered the best of conversation. I hadn't seen your mother in years, and I hadn't then met you. You may have preferred the quiet and beauty of the forest but you let me sit you on my knee and tell you stories.'

'Did I?' Elizabeth exclaimed, in temporary disbelief. Then after a moment she said, 'That is, I admit, vaguely familiar.'

'Vaguely familiar? We sat for hours telling stories. I'd tell you a story and when it was finished you wanted to hear another. I think that is how you first became fond of your old uncle Bartholomew.'

Elizabeth looked at him with an endearing smile. 'Yes I believe you are right. Did you tell me the story of the little girl who loved her pony so well that one day she climbed his paddock fence, slipped onto his back and without even a halter lead whispered to him to take her away for a very long walk? They went across the field and into a forest she'd never been before. Then they rode into a beautiful colourful flower filled meadow where she got off and picked flowers while her pony drank in the stream and enjoyed the thick grass.'

'Yes that was I', Bartholomew replied quietly. 'You remember the story well', he said sweetly, smiling at her.

'That is when I began to call you uncle', said Elizabeth in fond remembrance smiling back at him.

Evangeline had begun to scowl as she sat at the table. She felt she'd not been a part of the conversation, worse, she felt she could not relate. Why do they have this relationship she asked herself. She had been observing Elizabeth and listening to the two of them. They are close she said to herself. I can feel the warm rapport between them. He has an avuncular affection and love for her. And Elizabeth cares for him too. Yes they are close. And I am envious of their closeness. Why have I not this kind of relationship in my life? And a deep feeling of envy enveloped her. Here I sit, while not physically alone, emotionally completely out matched. These two people, not peers, have a warm relationship they both value. The maid was serving soup. She ladled the broth into Evangeline's Spode soup bowl and moved on to her neighbour. Evangeline, without interest mechanically picked up her silver soup spoon. The hot broth rather than warm her or satisfy hunger, seemed to spread as an infection a feeling of permeating discontent. Resentment filled her. She felt resentment for the lovely dinner service before them and for the service and the fine food they were given. It all filled her with envy and made the sitting at table almost unbearable. She put the spoon down. I feel empty, she said to herself. And the worst thing is I don't know how to change my life. I don't know how to change myself that I might have this kind, warm, uncomplicated love in my life. I don't know how to be more like Elizabeth. This feeling, envy, is present and overpowering. She studied Elizabeth. Her beauty, vitality, her happiness, makes me feel ill. She knows how to live, to enjoy life, to love. And I do not.

Evangeline sat, alone, amongst the others. And she thought to herself, I wish she were ill. I'd like to see the colour fade from Elizabeth's cheeks. I'd like to see her look worn and that smile die away. Evangeline felt hot and uncomfortable. She stood up, pushing her chair back and away from her.

'Are you alright?', Elizabeth turned to her guest, concerned.

Evangeline looked to the speaker. The question made her pause.

'I . . . don't feel well, I should be alright. Please excuse me I must get some air', Evangeline replied.

'Of course', Elizabeth said. 'May I . . . '

But Bartholomew had risen and gently placing his arm around Evangeline's shoulders said, 'I will escort you to the outside door closest to the garden. That is the quickest way to gain the outdoors', he said.

Evangeline wanted to refuse. She wanted to get away from this company.

But she heard herself say, 'Thank you.'

As she walked out of the dining room and into the hallway she felt Bartholomew's warmth and goodness there beside her, with her. And the dark hot pool of ill will for Elizabeth began to dissipate. Her cheeks felt less flushed. She turned her head slightly to see him beside her. His face was warm and kindly and there was concern in his eyes.

'You are very good . . . friends with Elizabeth?', she asked, though knowing the answer. Her voice was quieter than it had been just a few moments before.

'Yes. We are old, and good friends', he replied gently. And Evangeline heard the care in his voice. She felt ashamed. She felt ashamed of her own lack of understanding for life. She was ashamed that someone who only wished her well, Elizabeth, she had wished ill. She had wished Elizabeth ill because she herself had not found the way to be happier, to love and be loved. This man who was guiding her now, down the hall, that she might feel comforted and not alone, was doing so not solely out of gentlemanly courtesy. Evangeline was a guest at Tudor Court, a guest of Elizabeth's, and that meant something. She felt his genuine warmth and care. This is who he is. This is who a friend of Elizabeth's is. He would not know her feelings, the feelings she'd had just moments ago, of ill will. He would not know this characteristic of envy, which is part of who I am. He opened the door to the outside, she stepped out and he stepped out behind her.

'Have you been to the garden before?', he asked kindly, looking directly into her eyes.

'No', she said softly.

'This will be a lovely treat. This little path leads right to the garden. There are benches upon which to sit if you feel the need. It's a large garden, plenty to appreciate', he smiled into her.

'Thank you', she replied.

'Shall I come and look for you in a wee while?', he asked.

She paused. Then Evangeline replied, 'Thank you, that's very kind', she paused again. What she wanted to say was, 'Yes, yes please. Come and get me and take me away, where I don't know, just anywhere. I don't know anyone as kind and as good as you.' Instead she said, 'Thank you, but I'll be fine here. You must get back to the dinner. I will go into the garden as you suggest, it will do me good', and she managed a small smile.

She turned to the little path and began walking toward the garden. He waited a few moments watching her. She could feel him there, and sensed his care, though she did not turn around. In another moment she heard the door to the house close. And then she felt alone, though not quite as alone as she had felt half an hour ago sitting at table.

Evangeline crossed the threshold of the garden through the substantial wrought iron canopy made for its entrance. Walking slowly she breathed in the fresh clean air. The smell of the garden made her stop and look around. There was a bench by the hedge, she went to it and sat down. Bartholomew had been kind to her. And his kindness was the only kindness she'd experienced for as long as she could remember. But as Evangeline sat there and reflected she realised that that was not true. Elizabeth was kind. In fact, Elizabeth was the reason that she had experienced such kindness just now. Being in Elizabeth's home this kindness is naturally bestowed. In holding a barrier of envy against Elizabeth I could have easily excluded myself from this warmth. But Elizabeth's goodness was stronger.

She breathed deeply, the sweet scent of roses made her turn to look for them. Ahead as the path continued into the garden were rose bushes. Rich red roses, pure white, and peach colour roses, were planted together. She rose and walked toward them. Bending down to reach them Evangeline sniffed a sample of each different coloured flower. The peach and white roses had a more delicate scent. The rich red rose had a full bodied fragrance and she sniffed and sniffed. One of the red blossoms, full and perfect, had fallen from the bush and lay on the ground nearby. This one I can take with me she thought and stooped to pick it up.

Continuing her walk in the garden Evangeline kept the soft petals close to her nose and breathed in the rich sweet scent of the red rose. She found comfort in the soft touch of the petals and the scent of the flower. Passing the gardener's shed where climbers had been allowed to grow up the walls of the small structure, the fragrance from the little flowers on the vines made her stop.

'Oh Granny's garden', Evangeline said aloud, surprising herself. 'I remember now. She must have had the same plant in her garden. I haven't smelled that for years, not since I was a girl', Evangeline exclaimed speaking aloud to the plants. And as she stood before the vine tears came to her eyes. Memories of

Granny's garden, her house, the food Granny prepared for them, and Granny, flooded back to her.

There was a small bench a little way off from the gardener's shed. 'I may be able to still smell these little flowers from there', she whispered and went to sit. 'Yes', she exclaimed happily, 'I can smell them from here.' Breathing in, now much more attuned to the air around her, and taking in good deep breaths, Evangeline became more aware of everything. A vision of Granny's house came back to her. That little peaked roofed green house set amongst the trees with only a few other houses on the street, with an enormous old oak in the backyard, welcomed her for two weeks every summer.

Memories crowded in upon her. When Daddy drove up to the house I'd jump out of the car and take in Granny's lovely little front garden. 'The peonies were my favourites', she spoke aloud, not whispering anymore. 'Pink peonies, big and plump and full', and their fragrance came back to her. 'And there were snapdragons, they smelled so good too. I'd always rush up to the peonies first and stick my nose in them. Sometimes there was a bumble bee inside the flower and I'd have to look for another flower. I never wanted to shoo the bee away. Then I'd see the petunia's, always purple petunias, and I'd kneel down in the soft earth to sniff and sniff them. By that time Daddy had the suitcase out of the boot and would be bringing it up the walk. Sometimes Granny would have seen us and if she had she'd be out on the front porch smiling, happy to see Daddy and me. Sometimes a cousin might have heard the car drive up and would have run round from the big back garden to call to me,

'Evangeline, come round to the back, we're playing in the garden.' But Daddy would reply, 'Not yet dear, Evangeline will join you after her greeting with Granny.' And then I'd rush toward the porch if Granny was there. If Granny had not yet seen us I'd stop at the snapdragons for a good sniff whilst Daddy rang the bell and tried the front door. When Granny appeared she would throw her arms around me and I'd throw my arms around her which barely went halfway round her round tummy. And she'd ask how I was and tell me that my favourite oatmeal cookies were on the kitchen table. And I'd picture them with the tall glass and me waiting for her to pour out the milk. Oh how fresh and cold that milk was. Grandfather had been a lawyer and sometimes his clients couldn't pay him so they'd pay with what they had. A farmer gave them such wonderful milk, so tasty, and thick delicious cream. And that farmer kept bringing Granny that milk even after Grandfather died.

Daddy would leave my suitcase at the front door. I'd follow Daddy inside, we'd walk down the narrow hall to the kitchen. We'd sit down with Granny at the wood table and I'd have one of my favourite cookies that Granny had made. Granny would go to the fridge and then pour out my milk in that tall glass that was all ready on the table. I couldn't wait to drink it. So cold, so delicious. Granny and Daddy drank coffee and loved to talk together. After I'd finished my milk and two or three cookies I'd wait. I knew Granny wanted to look me over a few more times before she'd say, 'Go ahead dear, Emma or Arthur or George (which ever cousins were there), are waiting for you. Run along sweetie.' And I'd run out the back door and into her wonderfully fragrant garden.

It always seemed a long time but it was probably only an hour or so when Daddy would call from the back door. 'I'm going now dear.' And I'd run to the back door and into the house. Daddy would rub his hand on the top of my head and smile down on me. Evangeline paused in her revery, swallowing and choking back tears. For a moment, looking up from her place on the bench, she let these feelings take her beyond the moment. The substance of the memories carried her to a place beyond to where she had not lived for a long time. The memories reawakened the love that was their source. And this love was with her now again.

Daddy would walk through Granny's kitchen into the short narrow hall toward the front door and I'd follow behind. He'd pick up my suitcase and carry it up the stairs towards my room. Granny waited at the bottom of the stairs with her hand on the wood banister and would call up, 'Evangeline's room is the last door at the back of the house.' I always had the same room. I knew which room and Daddy knew which room it was that Granny had for me. Granny liked to say in this way, Evangeline loves the garden and that is the room that looks out on the garden. I loved that room, so quiet, so bright. I could always hear the birds chirping in the morning and at night. I'd stand on the little green sofa in front of the window with my elbows on the broad window sill and look out to the trees and grass and flowers. She always kept the drapes drawn completely back for me and I never closed them.

Evangeline stopped in her remembrance and became present to where she sat in Elizabeth's garden, tears streaming down her face. She hung her head and cried. 'Oh, what a wonderful childhood I had', she sobbed. 'How could I envy anyone else when I was so loved, so cared for. I'd forgotten all that. I've been bemoaning my state, I guess because life has changed. Granny's been gone such a long time. And Daddy is gone too. She paused, more tears filled her eyes. But Emma, and Arthur, and George are still alive. How awful of me to bemoan my life when I've done little, nothing really, to keep up such good relationships. A bird sang in a nearby tree. She looked up, it was a blue tit, a beautiful round blue capped yellow chested little bird. Granny had those in her trees. And she laughed at her childlike thought. Granny didn't have them. She made a place for them and they came to live. The sweet song of the blue tit was music to Evangeline. No one else could hear it. Evangeline listened and for the first time in her life she heard the blue tit's song.

Like the sun suddenly rising above the horizon announcing a new day, new and fresh thoughts of life arrived in Evangeline's mind. 'Elizabeth makes a place for neighbours, for guests, and for visitors here at Tudor Court. Elizabeth welcomes us, sort of like Granny. And I, instead of appreciating this, have envied her. And now I no longer envy. Evangeline rose from her seat and spreading her arms wide to the wonderful outdoors, spoke aloud. 'I love this place.' And she looked up to the sky where white clouds whisped across the blue. 'I love this life.' And the blue tit responded in chorus.

CHAPTER FOUR

THE CASE OF GREED

Greg Edgar is a greedy man. He is greedy for Elizabeth Fennington's connexions. Elizabeth's status in the community is of value to Edgar. He cannot miss an opportunity to advance himself, his holdings, and his bank account. He tries for an invitation to her soirées, parties, luncheons, and to the dinners Elizabeth gives. Edgar is careful not to over extend his welcome by avoiding pushing too hard. But he has almost missed the etiquette mark a few times. He feels he has the tennis parties as a good buffer, being rather rotund and short of breath, he does not play tennis and thus does not attend these parties.

Greg Edgar smiles a lot. And when he does it is a slow, sly, slightly slick, snake like line across his chubby face. He enjoys a laugh, sometimes at another's expense. But he is also the first to laugh along with another's good humour. His laugh is cleaner than his smile, perhaps because he enjoys life. His greed has made him a rich man, and he likes being rich.

Edgar's relish of his invitations and time at Tudor Court also arises from his love of comfort. The comfortable elegance of Tudor Court is to be admired, even appreciated. He enjoys luxuriating in the thick cruell work chesterfields and relaxing himself into the large deep set brocaded chairs whilst being served by one of Elizabeth's excellent servants. However the real value to Greg Edgar is the opportunity to be present with the moneyed class. And while not all of Elizabeth's guests are wealthy, they all have the connexions where Edgar knows how to make money.

On a warm June evening Elizabeth was giving a dinner party in honour of her friend's visit from America. Greg Edgar was invited and he duly accepted. Twelve sat at table. Edgar, seated across from the well known tycoon Wyatt Onwell, was listening attentively. Onwell was drilling a new oil well in Oklahoma and he was in the midst of looking for investors. Edgar was interested.

'If we strike oil you'll get your money with interest, and you'll get a cut of the profits', Onwell was telling Edgar.

'I've not invested in oil drilling. How does it work? The financial part I mean', replied Edgar.

'Ideally I like three other investors. We each put in a quarter of the money. I put in the know how as well. You get twenty percent of the profits. I get forty percent', he finished.

Greg Edgar's mouth was salivating. He swallowed, but feigned a flat expressionless face.

'Yes', he murmured.

'If you're interested, I'll ask Ann, my secretary, to send you over the details in the morning', Onwell offered.

'Thank you. I'll look for them in the morning', Edgar responded. His palms were sweating. His palms always sweated when he felt a good deal coming on. I'll probably have to invest two to three million, maybe something more. And my profit, his mouth was salivating again, would be four or five times that amount. It is true Edgar hadn't invested in oil drilling before. But he read voraciously about different industries and profit margins. And as he well knew the most important aspect of any business deal is the people involved. Do they know their area, are they honest, are they good experienced businessmen. Anyone at Elizabeth's table would be all three, the best.

The next day Edgar, instead of waiting for Onwell to send over the details, went to Onwell's office in London. Edgar had stayed up until 2:00AM thinking about the opportunity for making money. He was thinking about what his profit would be if he could be the only other investor. He was going to propose that he and Onwell be the only investors on the deal.

Edgar had to wait and Onwell's receptionist offered him coffee. Onwell was surprised to see him. He was quiet and watchful as he gestured Edgar to a chair by his desk.

'I hope you will approve of my boldness', Edgar said. 'I liked you when we met last evening. It seems we have an easy rapport. I was thinking that if it were just the two of us on the deal we'd have an easy time communicating and keep everything simpler.' Edgar stopped to gauge Onwell's reaction to the idea.

Onwell, looking at him, said, 'Go on.'

'I've worked out some figures.' He handed a sheet of paper across the desk to Onwell. 'As you'll see there', and he pointed to the bottom line, 'this way you'll have sixty percent of the profits instead of forty percent.'

Onwell glanced at the paper and then looked at Edgar, not taking his eyes off him now.

'And you'll double the profit you would have made', Onwell pointed out in a low voice without sarcasm.

Edgar smiled, that slow, sly, slightly slick smile of his, and said nothing. There was a pause as each man took the measure of the other.

Then Onwell said, 'As a matter of fact, an old friend called me early this morning to ask if I had anything going on and I told him of the well. He asked if he could be a part of it. I think your idea is a good one. I'm going to offer him the terms you've outlined here', he stopped.

Edgar felt his saliva dry up and his tongue stick to the roof of his mouth. The moments that passed until he could speak seemed interminable. He cleared his throat.

'Is there any room for me on this one?', as he spoke he quivered inside and his voice was soft and low.

Onwell responded immediately, 'I like your idea of just two of us on this deal. I've known my friend a very long time. It will be good to do this one together', is all Onwell said.

Edgar got up, wished Onwell well, and left the office.

As he walked into the street Edgar felt a shrinking of his stature. The feeling started from within, a cold crumbling wall that was his inner structure, the wall that kept him erect was collapsing. He couldn't bring himself to think about what had just taken place. A thought, unwanted but unavoidable, flited across his mind. If I'd not gone in there and just waited for the details he offered to send would I have my twenty percent profit?

And he sensed that it was his impatience displayed through his appearance in Onwell's office that changed Onwell's mind. And that impatience was spurred by what? Greed. Onwell was surprised to see me. Where he'd been pleased last evening to send me all the details this morning his surprise to see me made him wary. His friend probably had called. But he likely told him he'd have to wait to see what the other players he'd already spoken with would do. If they decided to go forward Onwell would have kept his word and his friend would have had to wait. But Edgar had disrupted the agreement by not waiting for Onwell's timing.

Twenty percent wasn't enough, I'd wanted forty percent. An hour ago I wanted forty percent so badly I could not even think of twenty percent. Now I cannot bare to think of the loss of twenty percent profit which would have translated into two or three million pounds. I can not bring myself to think about the fact that greed is my undoing. The acknowledgement would require the action of change. And that change can only come about through facing one's own nature. And that is a black curtain behind which I do not wish to peer.

Edgar had wandered up Fleet Street into Ludgate. He found himself staring up at the dome of St. Paul's. Some tourists brushed by him on their way to the Cathedral. Am I a fool, he asked of himself. I love to make money. Is that such a bad thing? Well, perhaps not. But I do feel poorly, very poorly indeed right now. Should money mean so much to me that it can bring on this malaise of spirit and physical symptoms, dry mouth, clammy palms? No, I'm sure not. And his head drooped, his chin almost touching his chest. More tourists brushed by him. He started to walk again.

He kept walking and subconsciously made his way to the train station where he could get his connection home. It was all a blur as he sat back in his seat on the train. Edgar stared out the window. The City and London had disappeared and he watched the countryside rush by. The long grass near the rail line waved at him. Goodbye to all that money. The farm houses further away, surrounded by neat and tidy grasses and gardens, looked cozy, friendly, compared to the City. He pulled his suit jacket a little tighter around him. As the train rushed forward, further and further from the City, he gradually let go of the dreadful feeling of loss he had experienced there a few hours ago. His mind went back to the previous evening and Elizabeth's dinner party. Why did I pay so little attention to the other guests? There were nine other people there, other than Elizabeth, to whom I paid very little notice. If I had given them even a little care I might now follow up with another opportunity. Now I'll never know what that could have been, he reprimanded himself. As soon as I heard of Onwell's opportunity my mind closed around it and closed out everything else. Is that all you are made of, a radar system to hone in on monetary matters? What about the rest of you? Another voice seemed to speak to Edgar from inside his head. Is there anything else to you? Edgar turned from the window to see his fellow passengers.

In the bank of seats directly across was a young woman, well dressed, perhaps twenty eight years of age, reading on her Kindle. She is quite attractive Edgar thought. She turned for a moment and smiled at him and then went back to her reading. He smiled, ever such a small smile but she had evoked a response. And nothing to do with money he said to himself firmly. He went back a moment in time, in reflection, to grasp a whisp of a feeling that had come in that smile. It was a very different feeling than he normally had. If he'd been able to see himself he would have seen that any trace of slyness or slickness in that smile was absent.

Edgar raised himself fully upright in his seat. In the seats directly in front of him were two older women who were happily chatting back and forth with one another. As he noted it now they had been doing so since the train started out of the station. He'd heard their voices until this moment only as background noise. He noticed that the conductor must have come along at some point as his ticket had been punched and placed at the back of his seat. That was four people of whom he'd not taken proper notice. There were more than twice as many last evening he'd not noticed either. At that moment the two older women broke out in laughter. He listened. And as he did, he thought to himself there is more to life than money. Yes of course there is. I used to know that. Mom and Dad knew that. They would laugh together quite a lot as I think about it now. They made for many happy times for all of us, at dinner each evening, vacations to the Lake District and the Cornish coast, and travels in Europe. What did I miss last night? Then another thought came to him. If Onwell tells Elizabeth of my greed, for that's what it is, greed, will she ever invite me to Tudor Court again? And Edgar didn't like that thought. Why has Elizabeth invited me in the past? I've never been the most sociable company. I've always had my ear open for just what I did last evening, opportunity to increase my fortune. Why has Elizabeth invited me? I'll have to come back to that one. I've not ever questioned as to why I was invited. I suppose I took it for granted that I'd be invited. And Edgar cringed at his own arrogance and lack of appreciation.

At least I've named it now. I am a greedy man. What is it about that that I do not like? I've enjoyed my fortune. I've earned it, or at least it's been made by me and my efforts. Perhaps I've not created much, but I've had a sharp eye and good business head and I've applied these. He moved restlessly in his seat. Why has Elizabeth invited me to Tudor Court? He thought back to the different times he'd been there. And while he recalled seven different occasions, he remembered little about them save the three particular people with whom he'd later engaged in business. It was all, it always had been, about money. He looked out the window again. The sun, slightly hidden behind a group of white fluffy clouds, streamed forth sunbeams down upon twenty or so sheep in the field beyond the railway tracks. 'How beautiful', Edgar spoke aloud. And at that moment he could see Elizabeth in his mind's eye. He saw her sunny smile beaming upon her guests. And there were special guests she'd have sit beside her with whom she'd laugh and talk. His neighbours in the seat in front of him broke out in laughter again. Through the separation between the two seats he could see the profile of one of the women. Her face was alight, her eyes, for all eighty years he guessed, were dancing with enjoyment in the conversation possible in the company of her friend. He'd seen this kind of enjoyment in Elizabeth when she engaged with her particular friends.

Why did Elizabeth include him at Tudor Court? This recurring question annoyed him. It annoyed him because an answer did not appear. In matters of making money there was a simple answer. How does £1000 become £1500? When £1,000,000 can become £1,500,000, invest. There was always a risk. But I've become reconciled to that risk and as a result of taking the risk, have, over time, made the profit. As he thought of the difference in outcome between himself and friends who had been distressed when they had lost money he smiled to himself. He'd been able to accept the reality. You have to be willing to take the risk. And he'd made a lot of money as a result. But he noticed that his smile didn't feel like the happy smile he'd been thinking about, Elizabeth's smile. And her laughter was of a different nature to his own. And he wondered about this. Why can I not see the reason Elizabeth includes me in her parties? I'm always thinking about money and investing. He paused. And I rarely think about other things, or other people. But Elizabeth does. Yes there is something there.

The following week Harold, Edgar's butler, handed Edgar his mail and amongst the letters was one from Elizabeth Fennington.

'I wonder . . .', Edgar said as he raised his brow and opened the envelope. 'An invitation to an afternoon tea' in a fortnight.

He smiled. Then to himself, how lovely of her. She knows. She knows that I went to Onwell's office, that he didn't perhaps trust me. She wants me to know I am welcome at Tudor Court.

I must respond by return post that I am delighted to attend. Edgar went directly to his writing desk. As he sat down he realised, Elizabeth is kind.

'What time shall I have the car for you Sir', asked Edgar's driver.

'Thank you Wallace. I shan't be needing it. I'll drive myself to Tudor Court.'

'Yes Sir', replied Wallace, somewhat surprised.

Wallace was surprised to see his employer near the garage. Edgar seldom walked this way. And Wallace had taken advantage of the opportunity to ask about the car. Edgar had recognised the surprise and chuckled to himself. Yes, my habits are changing.

And spontaneously Edgar turned around and said, 'You'll be seeing more of me about Wallace.'

Wallace nodded his head and said, 'Yes Sir, glad to hear it Sir.'

To himself Edgar noted, I'm enjoying spending more time on my estate. In the last three weeks I've taken a number of walks, walks I have not taken in years around my estate. He walked past the garage and onto the forest path leading to the south garden. A small bouquet is appropriate I think. He was a little excited with the prospect of picking the flowers himself and then presenting the posy to Elizabeth. The south garden had an abundance of colourful and fragrant flowers. Elizabeth's parlour, which is likely where the tea will be, is something of a neutral colour and I think there is some green, some pink, and some white. He was interrupted in his revery.

'May I assist you?', came an inquiring voice.

'Oh, hello', Edgar paused.

'I'm your gardener, or one of them', she laughed. 'I am Sabine', she took off her glove and offered her hand.

'How do you do?', Edgar shook her hand. He felt surprised with himself, feeling more friendly than annoyed at what he would have considered up until recently, a stranger's intrusion.

'Are you looking for something in particular?', she asked.

'Well, yes. I'd like to bring a small bouquet to my hostess for her tea. I was thinking of the parlour colours of neutral and green', Edgar offered.

'Fresh flowers will be welcome in any colour. If you will allow me?', she looked up at him as she bent over a bed of stock.

'Well . . . yes. Yes, please', Edgar replied.

In a few moments she'd travelled from one bed to another, expertly cutting with her gardener's knife a variety of flowers. She paused to survey the assortment. Holding the bunch away from her she rearranged a few stems and handed it to Edgar.

'A nice variety, yet not too many of different sorts, they match well colour and size wise', she smiled. 'Nice and fragrant too', she added.

'It looks lovely', Edgar said as he held the bouquet, appreciating her choices. He surprised himself again by sticking his nose in the posy. 'It smells divine', he exclaimed.

Sabine laughed and her eyes beamed at him.

'Thank you', Edgar said in a lower voice.

'You're very welcome', she smiled, and Edgar noticed it was a lovely bright warm smile. She bowed her head slightly and went back to her work.

'They are lovely,' Elizabeth responded brightly as Edgar handed her the posy. 'How thoughtful', she added. And then, as another thought came to her, 'Did you pick them yourself?'

'I did, with help from my gardener', Edgar responded, happy that his extra care had pleased his hostess. 'She explained that I need not match the colours of your room, which I had been seeking to do.'

Elizabeth laughed, 'Oh this bouquet is so lively, happy', and she looked happy.

'Morris, please choose a vase and bring the flowers back here', Elizabeth handed the bouquet to her housekeeper and patted the side table, indicating a place for the flowers to be near her.

I'm touched, Edgar said to himself.

When at tea, while the others were definitely engaged, Elizabeth leaned over to Edgar and said, 'Onwell went with an old friend of his on that opportunity. He is sometimes most meticulous, finicky, about all details of his business transactions. He know's this old friend well. And, he had just met you.' She looked at Edgar to learn his response. Edgar was listening attentively, gratefully. Then she added, 'Next time may be different', she gave him a kind, caring smile of understanding.

Edgar couldn't help but drop his head and look to his tea. He felt humbled, and gratefully so.

CHAPTER FIVE

THE CASE OF LUST

Leticia Ulster lusted after Elizabeth Fennington's life. Leticia was not the murdering kind, she lusted after the life Elizabeth led, including living at Tudor Court. Leticia took up tennis just to be available for the tennis parties at Tudor Court, which until she'd gained a modicum of skill in the sport, she'd had to forgo. Leticia canceled any engagement that got in the way of accepting a Tudor Court invitation.

Leticia needed to study Elizabeth. She was almost gluttonous for absorbing details of any little facet of Elizabeth's life. In Leticia's mind Elizabeth was living the perfect life at Tudor Court and Elizabeth was the model to emulate. What did Elizabeth wear? Where did she purchase her clothes and shoes? How was she wearing her hair? How did she speak? What were her topics of conversation? What was she thinking? Though an answer to this last question most often eluded Leticia.

Elizabeth and her life were the epitome of respectability and her person and life were to be admired. Elizabeth was beautiful, a gracious, even happy hostess. She dressed with exquisite taste, always the right outfit for the occasion. She had just the right word to include one of her guests when they were outside the conversation. Elizabeth knew how to begin and how to carry on a stimulating conversation. She could entice an entire room full of powerful and positioned people into an interesting and energized conversation. Once she'd done her magic she could leave the room if need be to return and find it filled with the sound of many voices all engaged, laughing, talking, with the feel too of people listening.

When at her first invitation three years ago Leticia had first seen the gardens and asked Elizabeth if she could take a walk in them Elizabeth had immediately assented and began to engage Leticia on gardening. Leticia confessed that while she was not a gardener she appreciated the beauty of a good garden. Elizabeth offered her a tour.

It was the tour of the garden with Elizabeth that made Leticia fall in love with Tudor Court. And this was when Leticia made Elizabeth her role model. Elizabeth's grace in sharing her secrets for a fine garden and her overall openness enchanted Leticia and acquainted her for the first time with life lived as Leticia imagined it should be. It was the beauty of the garden, the wild grasses, colourful flowers, and enormous old trees, that Leticia found so irresistably attractive. And with Elizabeth as guide Leticia began to learn how the garden came to be so beautiful.

Though Leticia had not seen it in this way, her life centred around her invitations to Tudor Court. Last year, when she had learned that Elizabeth would be away for three months Leticia fell into something of a depression. She could not imagine a month without the hope of an invitation to Tudor Court. Her calendar was prioritized around the party or gathering Elizabeth arranged. Leticia would look forward to thinking about who would be there, what she would wear, and what little treasure she would learn through Elizabeth. Afterwards, Leticia would go over in her mind the conversations she'd had, or those she'd heard. Sometimes she'd not understood what had been discussed and it bothered her to find herself excluded because she could not keep up. This concern occupied her as she considered at length how to improve herself.

Leticia recalled the last time she had been invited for dinner to Tudor Court.

'What will Elizabeth be wearing?', she spoke aloud to herself as well as to her maid.

'I didn't see Ellen in the village this week', Leticia's maid said.

'What was that? Oh, would Ellen have told you her mistress's plans for her wardrobe?', Leticia asked as she removed one dress or outfit after another from her closet and placed it up against herself to examine the effect in the mirror.

'Well Mamam, I don't ask her directly like', she paused.

Leticia stopped rummaging, 'How do you find out?'

'Well, I sort of flatter her mistress, with things like 'Miss Fennington knows all the right colours, skirt lengths, and whether to wear short or long sleeves, florals or solids, pumps or flats', Sarah smiled shyly as she enacted the imaginary conversation with Elizabeth's maid.

Leticia looking at Sarah and admiring her ingenuity asked, 'You've had this kind of conversation before?'

Sarah hesitated, 'Well, . . . yes . . . Mamam. You always seem keen on what Miss Fennington's wearing. How can I help if I don't find out?'

Leticia smiled and nodded but said to herself, am I that bad? Unbidden, my maid realises I'm mad to know what Elizabeth will wear, and seeks to find out. This time Leticia hesitated. But being unable to resist, asked, 'And do you know the hairdresser Miss Fennington uses?'

'Yes Mamam', Sarah replied promptly.

Leticia said simply, 'Yes?'

'It's Tailored Hair she goes to, off the high street.'

'And who there does she see?'

'Miss Laura, Mamam', Sarah replied.

'Very good. Thank you Sarah', Leticia let this last response mean both appreciation and a release. She gave Sarah a little smile and a nod before her maid exited the room.

Leticia quickly pulled a simple fawn coloured afternoon dress from the closet, changed into it, and left the room.

'Sarah, Sarah', she called to her maid.

'Yes Mamam', Sarah appeared from around the corner just catching sight of her mistress as she hastened down the stairs to the hall entryway.

'I'm going to the village. I'll be just an hour or so', Leticia spoke rapidly.

'Yes Mamam', Sarah replied as the outside door closed behind her mistress.

Leticia walked briskly along the high street. I'm not sure which side street Tailored Hair would be down she said to herself as she slowed her pace. Seeing a smartly dressed young woman looking in a shoppe window Leticia stepped forward.

'Excuse me, would you know of the hair salon, Tailored Hair?', Leticia asked and smiled at the bright eyed young woman who was now looking at her.

'Hello. Yes, yes I do. It is not this street', she gestured to the side street nearest them. 'Let me show you', and she led the way up the high street.

'Do you use Tailored Hair', Leticia inquired reservedly.

'I have done, yes. It's quite moderne', the young woman offered, and smiled.

'I've heard Laura is quite good', Leticia suggested.

'Laura is to whom I've gone. I don't live here. I'm visiting from London', she said.

'Oh', Leticia, chancing that this young woman might know Elizabeth, dove in with, 'I understand Elizabeth Fennington uses Laura and Elizabeth always looks so well turned out.'

'I know Elizabeth. When I'm here I help her with the museum she's trying to establish. In fact we just had lunch together after our meeting regarding the museum.'

Leticia almost jumped in with, 'How did Elizabeth look? What was she wearing? And what is she doing right now?' But she stopped herself thinking such a bombardment of questions unsuitable.

'She know's a lot of the local history and there's quite a bit of it', the young woman offered and introduced herself, 'I'm Charlotte Halsby', and Leticia's new acquaintance put forward her hand.

Having hoped she wouldn't have to divulge her name after using Elizabeth's so freely, she felt less mortified than might have been given her new acquaintance's open energetic manner and said, 'Leticia Ulster. How do you do?'

'Do you live here then?', Charlotte asked.

'Yes', Leticia nodded and smiled.

She stopped, 'Here it is, Tailored Hair', she said triumphantly.

Tailored Hair beckoned them with a clean white and green shoppe front, a large open paned window and a wood framed spotless large windowed wood door.

'Thank you very much you were most helpful', Leticia said.

'You're welcome. I'm off to get my train back to London. Cheerio', she smiled broadly.

'Goodbye', replied Leticia.

Leticia glanced inside the shoppe. It was fairly busy with three ladies under the dryers, one receiving a cut, and another a styling. No one I recognise and all the better, she said to herself. Thankfully my new acquantance having gone back to London, is now unlikely to speak with Elizabeth about my mention of Elizabeth's salon. Though it would be fine if my name is mentioned at a later date. Leticia smiled at the thought of Elizabeth hearing her name through a new source. Leticia went into the shoppe and made an appointment with Laura for the Friday. Then she drove back to her house imagining spending more time at Tudor Court.

When Elizabeth had gone off to Europe visiting friends and touring, Leticia truly at a loss, had begun some serious thinking.

Perhaps I have taken for granted how much of my enjoyment is centred in Tudor Court. This unawareness of from where my happiness comes is disturbing. It strikes me that I've been living merely waiting for my next visit to Tudor Court. In between these visits nothing of import takes place. Time with a friend, shopping, rearranging the furniture, or something unexpected to do with the upkeep of the house is the sum total of my time. As I think about it I do not have a friend I enjoy anywhere near as much as I enjoy being in the company of those at Tudor Court. And Leticia became a little worried at this revelation.

Why have I not recognised my situation before? Why am I only now stopping to think? Why is Tudor Court so important to me? It is there that important people gather. I feel important when amongst them. Nowhere else do I find myself in such company. Why do I feel that these people are important, superior really to others I meet? They are educated, most more than myself. Yet I have an undergraduate degree from an acceptable university. Most of those I meet at Tudor Court have at least a masters degree, some a doctorate, some more than one doctorate. All are world travelled. But I have travelled. As a senior executive with a large international company Father had included us on some of his trips. Mum's small but successful craftware company did well in North America. She had brought European original and cultural design to simple everyday products like water pitchers, dining and bedroom linens, dishes, and dishware. Italian, Portuguese, and French designs she had had made for the North American wealthy niche markets in San Francisco, Los Angeles, Chicago, New York, and Toronto. I travelled extensively with my parents in Europe and North America. Mum always took me to the museums and art shows. Over the years I learned a lot about art and I know what I like. I was thrilled when I realised I could hold my own at Tudor Court when conversations were about art.

What else makes these people at Tudor Court superior in my eyes? They have good taste. Their dress, manners, knowledge of art, combine to good taste, and I relish good taste. But as I think about them none of them have sought with kindness to relieve my feelings of inadequacy and ultimately feelings of exclusion when I was unable to carry the thread of conversation.

Leticia paused in her thoughts about those whom she'd met at Tudor Court and a feeling of inadequacy came rushing back to her. This feeling along with the feeling of being excluded, naturally excluded perhaps, made her feel unhappy and very uncomfortable. As she thought about her most recent visit where she'd experienced these feelings she realised that it was not the first time she had felt uncomfortable. It was a natural consequence of at some point not being able to follow the train of conversation and getting lost and left behind. But no one, not once, had stepped in to help her. Why? Had no one noticed? It didn't seem possible. If they had noticed why would not someone bring me aside, why wouldn't someone speak with me to bring me back into the conversation? There was no one there with the kindness to do so. Then Leticia thought of Elizabeth. Elizabeth was kind. She continued in her revery. As I think about it Elizabeth had not been a part of these conversations. Had Elizabeth been there she would have ensured that I was not excluded. She would have found a way to bring me back into the conversation. Leticia felt alone. Elizabeth, whom she could not even call a friend, had behaved as a friend. Not having recognised from where her happiness came made Leticia feel more alone in the world. She got up from the green and yellow chesterfield in her sunroom and went through the French doors that led to the back garden.

What is this state I am in? I have placed so much value on Tudor Court and haven't even realised it. Instead of being hurt and feeling excluded by people not kind enough to consider me, I should be angry, or put off by this behavior. And she let herself think about this as she meandered in her garden.

Over the time Elizabeth had been away these recurring thoughts gave Leticia opportunity to consider her preoccupation with Elizabeth and Tudor Court. Now as Leticia made her dinner she continued her reflection. In some way she was letting go of the hold Tudor Court and its guests had upon her. But the appeal Elizabeth had remained. Why did Elizabeth go to all the trouble of arranging and holding parties? Did Elizabeth enjoy her guests? Leticia thought about this over her dinner. She tried to recall seeing Elizabeth in her mind's eye with her guests. And she could not recall a scene where Elizabeth was engaged for any length of time with any group of guests nor any individual guest. Then she realised, that while Elizabeth was always present to welcome a guest's arrival she did not always engage with her guests but to introduce them to one another. If necessary she would initiate a conversation for them simply to encourage their comfort together. Why Leticia thought, did Elizabeth give these parties?

As the charm and appeal of the Tudor Court guests began to dissipate the appreciation Leticia held for Elizabeth increased. As she contemplated her so oft hostess a face appeared in her mind's eye, Bartholomew Atwater. Bartholomew Atwater had been a visitor to Tudor Court. A visitor was differentiated from a guest in that he or she usually stayed at Tudor Court. Guests came and left. Elizabeth included visitors with her guests every so often. And these she did engage. Leticia scrutinized Batholomew Atwater's face as it appeared in her mind's eye. It was an animated face full of life, expressive, and responsive in an uncommon way. There was something about that responsiveness that caught Leticia's attention although she did not know what it was. A far greater interest than the one Leticia yet had would be required to grasp the meaning of that something in Batholomew Atwater's face that caught her attention.

Bartholomew Atwater's responsiveness, so appealing to the observer, so valuable to the friend, had the rare quality of understanding. There is nothing quite like being understood. A great deal of love is required to understand another. When someone responds and knows why they respond to you as they do, when someone understands and appreciates who you are, that is divine.

When Leticia awoke the first thing she did was go to her calendar for the upcoming Tudor Court invitation. This time her anticipation was not for the guests rather it was to better understand Elizabeth and the difference between Elizabeth's visitors and her guests. She would learn something about Elizabeth in a different way this time. This time she wanted to learn something important, something telling of who Elizabeth is, something worth learning.

Leticia Ulster and Arnold Abercrombie both arrived at Tudor Court at the same time and were seated in the parlour. Moments later Elizabeth wafted into the room in a beautiful sea green dress that hung perfectly accentuating her graceful figure.

'Thank you for coming', Elizabeth said in her warm clear voice offering genuine welcome.

Arnold rose upon her entering the room and Leticia intuitively followed suit.

'Please', Elizabeth gestured to the door, 'let's go to the smaller drawing room where Morris will have the tea laid out for us', her voice was full of energy as though Spring had arrived along with her. One didn't want to miss a moment. And one's feet seemed to skip to the rythym of life to which Elizabeth danced.

The other guests, already seated, sat on highbacked Georgian chairs and on two small sofas with the tea laid out between them on two Spanish style pale wood coffee tables. The tea consisted of perfect cucumber and watercress sandwiches along with hot scones, Devon cream, and scrumptious homemade strawberry jam (Mary Lemes's, Elizabeth's cook, great grandmother's recipe). Arnold, evidently pleased with the presence of three of his neighbours, initiated the conversation.

'Are you involved in the effort to stop the council's move to expand public access to the walking paths, and to paving them?', Arnold asked Edwin Barth.

'I am. They are trying to push it through and they should not be spending the money', Edwin responded.

Joana Lester added, 'The plan they have would expand the path far into the fox hunting area, and that has got a lot of our country neighbours het up.'

'The local judicial body has asked me to oversee the Northumberland North council communication with the county legislative body on the matter', said Samuel Remington. And he began a discourse on the latest news on the subject in which all were interested.

Elizabeth had poured out the tea. Now that her guests were well underway, voicing their views and getting to know their neighbours better, Elizabeth, noticing that Leticia was not involved, addressed her guest, 'Would you like to take a tour around the house?', Elizabeth asked thoughtfully. 'I know you have seen many of the rooms but sometimes a tour can be fun', she smiled. 'I think they are well underway', Elizabeth said looking to her guests who were much engaged, 'come, let me start you off', she said as she stood and then moved to the doorway. 'Just around the corner is my favourite room.' Elizabeth enticed Leticia, who though surprised, was delighted by her hostess's gesture and had followed her out of the drawing room and forward into the hall.

Elizabeth opened the large oak wood door for Leticia to enter, 'This is the library.'

Leticia walked into a spacious, open, high ceilinged oak panelled rectangular room filled with natural light.

'The oak panelling helps insulate the room from any external sound. It's quite wonderful to be here reading a good book. One can be quite absorbed, taken away where the author would lead', she spoke with the simple happiness and enthusiasm of a child who is in the throes of her favourite stories.

Leticia walked to the enormous windows at the other end of the room.

'Is this part of the garden the windows face?', she asked.

'Yes. This is the south end of the garden. The light is from the southwest here. So there is good light all day even in the winter. I can come here at all times during the day and read with natural light', she smiled, happy to share one of her delights in life.

'Do you read a lot then?' Leticia asked.

Elizabeth paused, 'Yes, I suppose I do.'

The walls were lined with books, fiction arranged alphabetically by author as were her favourite non-fiction authors (as example, Jacques Barzun, Winston Churchill, and C.S. Lewis). Otherwise non-fiction was arranged by subject. There were over ten thousand books, Elizabeth did not have a count. She noticed that Leticia did not peruse the shelves to learn what books were on treasure. She was about to ask if Leticia enjoyed reading but the question had perhaps been answered.

'What would you like to see?', Elizabeth asked instead. When no answer was given Elizabeth said, 'Perhaps you would enjoy wandering, you are welcome. Then you can be at your leisure. I will have to get back to my guests. They will notice me gone and may want more tea or scones', Elizabeth said with a happy lilt in her voice.

'Thank you. Would that be alright?' Leticia asked, thrilled to be able to spend the full extent of her curiosity.

'Yes. Enjoy yourself. The house isn't that big. But should you get lost, you're bound to run into Chalmers or Morris the housekeeper, and they can direct you. And if you feel like fresh air and a stroll in the garden go right ahead. There is a door to the outside right along the passage', she smiled.

'Thank you', Leticia bubbled in response to Elizabeth's kind thoughtfulness.

Elizabeth turned and retraced her steps toward the drawing room.

I'm tingling inside being able to wander freely as though Tudor Court were my own house. Leticia almost spoke aloud in her excitement. I've seen the entryway, the Great hallway with the enormous hearth leading to the rest of the house, the parlour, library, and drawing room. Perhaps I can find the other drawing room and the Great Room. Arnold said there are fifteen rooms. I mustn't go up to the bedrooms. That leaves the old men's smoking room, perhaps I can pop my head in there. I wonder for what she uses that room. Then there is the dining room of course. There must be another room, perhaps a den, an art room or even a council chamber. The dining room I've seen but would like to see again on my own. The large drawing room should be off the dining room as would be the smoking room. And the Great Room could be elsewhere. Leticia heard someone speaking, she guessed it must be one of the servants.

'Yes Mamam, Reggie delivered the groceries at 11:00 like they'd said they'd a done.'

'Is the baking underway?', the cook was asking.

'Yes Mamam. I just put both the cakes and pies in the ovens now', she replied.

'Good girl Cathy', came the response.

That must be the cook speaking to her helper. Leticia felt a pang of jealousy as she realised that Elizabeth would again be entertaining for dinner. How can I expect to be invited? I'm here now, invited to tea. And, she reminded herself, invited to wander and explore at will this wonderful home. She turned down the hall that appeared before her.

Leticia came upon the dining room and stopped and stood in the entryway. The long rectangular wood, French she thought, table, was beautifully set for eight, for something of an intimate dinner Leticia thought. It was set with soup bowls and two sets of plates, salad and main course. An exquisite silver candelabra was the centrepiece and a colourful bouquet of stock, snapdragons, and greens in a burgundy and clear glass crystal vase graced that part of the table close to where the guests would be seated. The dining chairs were tall backed and looked to be of cherry wood with tapestry like damask cushioned seats in subdued gold and deep red. 'Beautiful. I loved the chairs the first time I experienced a dinner here. I've not seen anything like them, Leticia continued talking to herself. 'I wonder where Elizabeth found them.' There was one large broad window at either end of the room. Each window was draped in an off white background with a medium green and light brown simple pattern in a substantive cotton which was flung back against the walls letting in all the light. 'What a beautiful room', Leticia exclaimed aloud. And to herself, I'm sure the food will be excellent. And the fine dress of the guests will accentuate the beauty of the room. What a lovely ambiance in which to enjoy fine dining with pleasant and interesting dinner companions. Leticia sighed. She sighed again on leaving such a beautiful room. She sighed a third time as she moved down the hall registering a pang of regret for being unable to assuage the desire to be included in the evening party. Then her new thinking that the greater value lay in knowing Elizabeth than in competing with Tudor Court guests returned to her. Slowing her pace as she walked the hall Leticia thought, 'This is Elizabeth's home and I can learn from being in her home and observing how she lives for surely she has chosen all this and it is a reflection of her.' As she moved down the halls Leticia looked from side to side taking in all the beauty of painting, rug, lamp, vase, wood paneling and ceiling mouldings.

The adornment of the hallway walls was far from typical. Rather than country hunting scenes, family portraits, or still life's, there were original paintings, sketches, and woodcuts. Leticia's attention went to a number of impressionist type paintings. 'Elizabeth likes colour and this style of work leaves a lot for the imagination', Leticia whispered. 'She likes what I like in painting', Leticia almost squealed. She came upon a large rectangular painting, its scene vertically oriented sitting like a large mirror on the wall. The painting depicted a garden scene in greens and yellows and pinks with what might have been Monet's house at Giverny in the background. In the foreground was the gardener crouching by, and almost hidden by, a large bush. Elizabeth had placed it across from a window. At that moment the light from the window falling on the painting seemed to be sunlight in the garden of the painting. Leticia stood looking into the scene. And while with a little more imagination she might have been momentarily transported by the artist's, Edouard Vuillard, genius, she ably appreciated the beauty.

Leticia continued along the hallway. The thick Turkish carpets beneath her feet were placed about two feet from the walls on either side. This displayed the well kept wideplank oak hardwood beneath. There were few decorative objects and no ornamentation in the halls. While there were pieces of furniture; a beautiful chair, an unusual console table, an elegant side board type wood piece, an exquisite lamp, the house itself well planned and well built stood in all its substantive strength unfettered, a fine representation of English country life.

Leticia passed a few doors that she suspected were cupboards and closets for the servants use for storing articles of linen and other dining room accoutrements or for items used for cleaning. Then she came upon the large drawing room. I've been in this room she said to herself. She paused in the open entryway. 'What a charming room', she whispered. The proportions of the room seemed to fit its purpose. And now Leticia seeing the room without guests felt the purpose Elizabeth must have in mind. She wants to offer her guest a comfortable, warm, welcoming, place for encouraging good conversation after dinner. The large armchairs were drawn in close to the two large big cushioned chesterfields and all were positioned in front of the enormous open fireplace. A little further off there were two sets of large armchairs positioned on either side of the fireside for more intimate conversations. And should others wish to join, straight back chairs against the wall could easily be moved into position for conversation.

Off to the side of one of the chesterfields a large circular table held a tall crystal vase with an abundant array of fresh cut flowers. Beyond the table four spacious armchairs offered a separate place for guests seeking privacy.

'I'd like to plop myself down right here and take an afternoon nap on this luxurious chesterfield', Leticia whispered to herself as she ran her hand along the back of the well stuffed furniture piece in deep green's and pale yellows.

'I think I'd dream of this wonderful house as my own and of all the guests who'd come to see me to appreciate its beauty.' As she was reluctantly about to leave the drawing room, Leticia noticed a two sided wall panel which looked so much a part of the wall that it was almost missed. Going up to the paneling to take a better look Leticia could see two separate panels. She slid each side back into its recess, revealing the old men's smoking room. Suddenly she felt drawn into another time, a time long gone by. The darker colours of the walls and furniture made for a more manly room, a room made for men who spent time talking and smoking good cigarettes and very good cigars. This room was where men had talked together about an imperial England that now no longer existed. Leticia walked slowly around the edges of the room, not comfortable with the heavy dark furniture and the vacant corners.

'Elizabeth doesn't use this room', she said quietly to no one there. And then Leticia drew the wood panelled doors back in place.

She continued down the broad hallway passing a door leading outside.

'I want to see the gardens', Leticia said aloud, but I'll complete my tour first she thought. The end of the hallway widened out and led into the Great Room.

The Great Room, of an enormous rectangular shape, was at the end of the house. The walls and ceiling at its far end were almost completely window and skylight combined. In mid afternoon the room was flooded with light.

'What an unusual Great Room', she exclaimed aloud. There was no one to hear her. 'As one walks toward the far end it feels like one could enter a garden paradise. It could be a great botanical atrium if one introduced plants.'

Leticia walked slowly to the centre of the room and took in the stunning beauty all around her.

'The hair on my arms is standing up – the high ceilings, the gleaming wood floor, and the beautiful ancient Roman motif mouldings along the juncture of walls and ceiling – such beauty such simplicity', she spoke aloud in a low awed voice. 'Elizabeth is exactly right in not having anything extra to detract from the room's beautiful design.' Leticia recalled a friend telling her that almost immediately upon taking possession Elizabeth had offered pieces of furniture to her neighbours. And, that over the course of a week there had been more vehicles coming and going in Tudor Lane than had visited for years. 'It's obvious', as she stood surveying the entire room from its centre, 'she must have removed a number of chairs and tables. And I would have left them thinking the room would feel bare. What Leticia had thought would be bare was to Elizabeth clean and open and beautifully simple. In fact Elizabeth had removed from the Great Room all the chairs, the paintings, and all the heavy dark drapery. The windows which had been made to be almost floor to ceiling now bore sheer cotton drapes inviting in all the light. The light in the Great Room was as being outdoors and well worth any natural fading of the floors with time.

As Leticia stood quietly absorbing the beauty surrounding her the reason for her love of Tudor Court dawned upon her. Tudor Court embodied history and the aristocracy, romance and glamour. Leticia said aloud, 'At night the moon and the stars must visit. Oh what a wonderful place for dancing', and the thought of this brought a full smile to her face. Surprising herself she said aloud, 'I must get back to the other guests.' Something about all the beauty she had experienced the last half hour moved her to a more gracious perspective.

Leticia moved back out into the hallway and took another long last look at the Great Room. As she walked slowly along the hallway she was tingling again. What a privilege to have this time to explore and discover her favourite place as though it were hers alone. Having a slow walk through Tudor Court's quiet hallways she had learned something more of Elizabeth, something of her depth was reflected in her classic sensibility. Leticia turned decisively down the hall to return to the drawing room. She looked out the windows as she passed and seeing the garden said aloud, 'I hope Elizabeth will have me back and that we may again have some time together in her garden.'

Letticia moved quietly as she approached the drawing room. Chalmers was hovering in the hallway and approached silently to open the door for her. She stepped softly into the room. Arnold Abercrombie, Samuel Remington, and Edwin Barth were engrossed in a three way conversation. Joana Lester and Elizabeth were listening. Elizabeth looked up and smiled, patting the seat beside her for Leticia to take. In a moment the slight guilt of selfishly having wanted to tour the house and ignore her social obligation left her. As she sat beside Elizabeth feeling warmly welcomed back, Letticia felt fully part of the afternoon ensemble and the comfort this gave encouraged reflection.

Elizabeth had chosen these guests to match each other's sensibilities. Three men, three women, all single, independent business men, independent women. While I wouldn't have given up that, private and secretly exciting in its self directed independence, tour of Tudor Court, I do feel pleased to be welcomed back to this comfortable little unit. It is Elizabeth that makes one so comfortable. Elizabeth is filled with just the right sense of responsibility for her guest. No. It is more than that. Elizabeth does the right thing. She has invited her guests and she intends to work for their comfort and complete enjoyment, just as she did for mine so particularly. Elizabeth was not simply obliging me, she truly wanted my enjoyment. As a result she could see what that enjoyment would be. When Elizabeth asked me if I'd like to tour the house she had done so knowing what would make my visit just right. And Leticia sighed aloud again. Elizabeth turned to her with a smile and an upraised brow as if to ask, 'Yes?' Leticia returned the smile and gave a slight shake of her head. Elizabeth, ever aware and attentive of her guests, turned back to the group.

Late that afternoon Leticia sat quietly in her own parlour. She had chosen, not her favourite cushioned chair, rather a straight backed chair she normally avoided. Rather than calling a friend to share the delight and the details of her visit to Tudor Court, which she often had done after returning from her favourite place, she felt a need to collect herself. She had enjoyed the afternoon very much. Leticia had also learned something about herself and she recognised she had learned through Elizabeth. As she sat quietly Leticia sought to grasp the meaning in what she had learned. Her over fascination, her obsession really, with Elizabeth Fennington had today worked to her advantage. Her attention to Elizabeth had resulted in an awareness of her own character. Leticia now reflected upon the quality of Elizabeth's character and how it provided opportunity for insight into her own.

A recognition of character can be a most sobering realisation especially when it is of one's own character. 'I have lusted after the things of Elizabeth, Tudor Court in particular. But Tudor Court is a house made a home by Elizabeth, through her care, warmth, and interest. While an especially lovely house with an unusual lustre given its setting, history, and the sense of life it embodies, Tudor Court is a representation of that which I have been trying to grasp, to have as my own. At what am I grasping? Leticia sat very still as she tried to see through the fog in her mind. There was something there, vague though it was, she must wait for it. It was when I thanked Elizabeth and was leaving Tudor Court that I sensed that there was something new, some new understanding within me. That's why when arriving home I walked past the telephone and into the parlour to sit, and to wait. I have lusted after what Elizabeth has, material things, the attention of others and those others whom I have deemed superior in some way. And now in this recognition I feel disappointment. It is disappointment for setting myself so low, for setting myself at that which has no real worth. But perhaps, there is a glimmer of something there which is of great value, something sensed, not seen, and unfortunately, not understood. I have a chance to understand it now. What is it? She waited.

Leticia continued to sit very still looking out the large parlour window to her garden. A sparrow alighted on a branch of the old oak tree just outside the window. She raised her line of vision to watch him. The sky beyond was blue with lovely white fluffy clouds moving slowly, steadily, westward. Sunbeams streamed through the clouds toward the earth at a distance closer to the horizon. Beautiful. The sparrow, still perching on the branch, chirped. Leticia smiled, he is enjoying this evening too. And then it came to her as the sun rising suddenly illuminates the landscape. It's simply the being, being present to life. Life is all around us. It's not the things in life. It's being alive to life and appreciating life. The most natural thing is to be oneself, be present, and make the most of every moment. 'The plain grey sparrow is a fine example', she spoke aloud. That is Elizabeth's secret. She is so very alive to life. This is what she shares with all who come to Tudor Court, a simple profound interest in life. In so being she creates room, a lot of room, for life. And Tudor Court is the place where she does this. And one can easily mistake the place, the where, when one should be seeing the 'who'. Elizabeth understands something about life, something at the essence of life. In experiencing this care, this understanding Elizabeth has for life, being in her presence, others feel more alive. She helps others to step into that special space and be more of who they are.

The sparrow continued to sit on the branch of the oak tree as Leticia watched. He is free, she thought. And with that thought, he flew into the sky and she watched him wing his way skyward. Leticia stood raising her face to the sky. Then, with a slight nod of her head, and a bow of her body to the grandeur of life she spread her arms wide and a joyful smile lit her face.

CHAPTER SIX

THE CASE OF VANITY

Vernon Athiny was so vain that he always carried a spike tipped umbrella in case he dropped his monogramed white handkerchief. That is, he could not deign to stoop to pick it up. He'd rather risk putting a hole in his hankie if he missed the little loop sewn in for use with the umbrella tip. If by chance all his hankie's were being laundered, forced to use a tissue and if per chance that tissue should drop from his hand or pocket, he would stoop. For he could not walk on for fear of someone seeing him and thinking him a litterer. He was too vain to have any such imperfection associated with his person.

Mr Athiny's perfect posture held him fully and firmly erect, his back as straight as a board, his head held high, his nose in the air, his shoulders back. He regularly glanced from side to side to learn if anyone was watching. He presumed many would notice and then watch him for he considered himself handsome. His tailored suits were Saville Row, he invariably wore Church's brogues always polished to a gleaming shine, and his coiffure was maintained by Louis the gentleman's barber. Louis was an old barber from London who kept a shoppe in Cirencester high street for particular clients. Athiny visited Louis every three and a half weeks without fail.

Vernon Athiny was single, he had never married. He had contemplated matrimony in his youth at the age of twenty five when the blush of romance held a sweet entrancement to his mind. But meditation on marriage, a long lasting, forever endeavour, moved his mind quickly from a feeling of romance to a pedantic feeling without a blush to savour. And so Athiny attended Elizabeth Fennington's parties alone, never flirting, always perfect in dress and always behaving with the utmost decorum. He liked to be seen with the right people. The right people were those who also knew how to dress, how to speak, what to say and what not to say, who were cultured, and who had money.

'You can have the night off if you like', Vernon said to his cook Atwell.

Atwell was the only servant Vernon Athiny kept. Perhaps this was because Vernon was so very particular. Everything, from the floors to the doorknobs and up to the chandeliers must be perfect. Few could keep his standard. He had hired and fired he knew not how many housekeepers, seven valets, and four drivers over the years. It was easier to reprimand the cleaners he employed on monthly contract as they went home at the end of the day. He was his own best valet. He knew his clothes and their upkeep far better than anyone else was even capable of knowing. And he liked driving his Porsche, his Land Rover, and his Audi himself.

Atwell was an excellent cook and Athiny liked to eat well. But tonight he'd dine with Elizabeth Fennington and her guests at Tudor Court. And that would be a very good dinner indeed. Atwell was probably a better cook than Mary Lemes, Elizabeth's cook. But Mrs Lemes had her specialities which Atwell did not make. And Tudor Court was a particularly fine manor house with splendid grounds perfectly nestled into the surrounding landscape. Athiny, liking to remind himself of Tudor Court's charm before a visit, tingled inside with anticipation. The drive into the Tudor Court grounds was especially beautiful. After one takes the bend in the road the house appears, perfectly set, as though painted into the landscape. The trees part to give one one's first glimpse of the stately house in all her glory. The size of the house, just the right size, its natural grandeur and its ancient stone, make one feel that Tudor Court will stand amongst its ancient copper beech trees, forever.

And there were the Tudor Court guests. After returning home following his first visit, an afternoon tea, Athiny had been so thoroughly impressed that he sat down immediately at his Louis XV writing desk to record the event. He knew he'd be impressed with the house and grounds but he had not appreciated what his response would be to the guests.

There had been four others, besides Elizabeth, at tea. Sitting beside him was an ancient grand dame, a Northumberland matron, Dame Catherine Wentworth. Athiny had heard of her of course. But to be sitting with her, let alone beside her at tea and only six of them all together, was an event to savour. Instantly, even before introductions, he had recognised her necklace as Cartier, with much history behind it for he knew it to be from the early nineteenth century. It was beautifully and simply set with perfectly matched pearls of exquisite lustre. He had tried not to stare.

She had turned to him simply to ask for the strawberry jam but after he had passed it to her she asked about Atwell, his cook of all things. Apparently at some point prior to coming to Athiny Atwell had been engaged in the household of Dame Catherine's brother.

'I can honestly say, I have not ever tasted a more delicious vegetable soup than that which Atwell prepared.' These had been her exact words. And these he had recorded in his diary. Then to his great surprise and infinite delight she had asked if there was any chance she could borrow Atwell for an evening to prepare that soup at her home. Dame Catherine had made it most clear that it was for a special occasion or she would not think of asking.

'The Earl of Hazelmoor is coming for dinner. I know how he enjoys a good soup. If Atwell is secretive about his recipes I will ask my cook to attend at the other end of the kitchen whilst he makes his preparations', she had said.

'Oh no I'm sure Atwell would be happy to share his recipe. He so enjoys it when someone appreciates his cooking', I said in return. Athiny had duly recorded their conversation. Athiny had been beside himself after the tea imagining the further contact he'd have with Dame Catherine in follow up for the lending out of his cook. Thinking about what favour she might grant or gift she might bestow in repayment for leaving him without a cook for an evening delighted him even in his dreams.

For a month following the tea he had shamelessly dropped names, Elizabeth Fennington, Tudor Court, and most often Dame Catherine Wentworth. He had audaciously used the cachet of Tudor Court and Dame Catherine Wentworth with his neighbour Henri Banally who had but given him the time of day once in all the years they had bordered each other's property. The moment he thought of the idea of needling his neighbour Athiny shot over in his sport's car with the made up excuse of asking Banally's advice on some legal matter. While in conversation he dropped the names. Banally's normally gruff exterior, lawyerly intellectualism, and snobby manner melted away like an ice cube in the Florida sun. Athiny had sought merely the enjoyment of batting Banally where he'd least expect it. He got much more than he bargained for, he found himself invited for a drink. What was even better was finding that Banally's snobbery was without foundation. The house was smaller than his own, the furniture and carpets imitations, and the artwork really nothing of which to speak. Banally had merely a few nineteenth century unknowns, whereas Athiny had a Chagall and a Picasso.

Athiny was very much looking forward to the evening at Tudor Court. The invitation to dinner was always formal arriving three weeks prior to the invitation’s date. Athiny had instantly recognised Elizabeth's distinctive paper. He enjoyed handling the thickness and texture of the envelope, the off white cotton textured paper felt smooth and soft in his hands. The invitation was hand written in Elizabeth's upward and forward sloping open style. If not for its elegance the invitation would have looked cheerful.

Athiny laid out his finest new shirts just in from his tailor. Finkleman and Sons ordered Athiny's shirts from Hong Kong where the shirt makers had his measurements and used the finest cottons from Egypt, India, and the United States. Then he went to his suit closet to choose the suit for the evening. Athiny scrutinized the Saville Row row of suits hanging in order of colour, lightest to darkest. He hesitated at the grey green one, the most lively suit in his Saville Row collection. I feel slightly daring he said to himself and closing the closet door went across the hall to the neighbouring room. He switched on the light, went to the closet, and opened its perfectly painted white French doors. Athiny smiled, here were his extravagances. While these suits he rarely wore, he just loved owning them. And tonight he would chose one to wear to Tudor Court.

There were ten suits in all, all purchased in Athiny's travels. Seven he'd purchased in New York in the last seven years. And he reached for this group. He fingered the fine wool of the dark grey suit he'd found at Barney's. But it was July and too heavy a material for this time of year. He sighed and cast his eye over the rest of his collection. Then he saw it, the lighter than navy blue silk suit made in Italy by that unknown artist. The man was truly an artist Athiny had decided. The sales woman at Bergdorf Goodman had told him the story behind that suit and its maker. She must have been eighty, she had been personally trained by Mr Goodman. She was so knowledgeable Athiny had been surprised that she was out on the floor. While finding him just the right suit and fit she had told him she was the men's Italian buyer. And she came out on the floor one day a month to keep in touch with the customer. He didn't try on any other suit for she had sized him up, not only physically, but personally. She had gone to the back and brought out one suit for him, this suit.

'This is your suit', is all she said.

Normally Athiny would not have hesitated, he would have said immediately no it's the wrong colour. But he had hesitated. This woman knew her business and he respected her aplomb. He gave her a nod and while she led him to the dressing room she told him about the maker of the suit. He was young, yet unknown, but he had an eye like no other.

'You can see for yourself', she'd said.

After he'd stepped into the pants she remarked, 'Look how the cut and fabric hangs on you.' And she had been right. It was as though the tailor had been making Athiny's suits for years. The pants were a perfect fit.

'What is the fabric?', Athiny had asked.

'A unique blend of silk and cotton. It is his own design.'

She had held the jacket for him. If it fit, he wouldn't even ask the price, he'd take it. The jacket seemed to reshape his narrow shoulders. Athiny had always felt self conscious of his narrow shoulders, feeling them to be unmanly. But beneath the magic mantel this tailor had woven Athiny felt uplifted. Thrusting his shoulders back he saw himself smiling in his new found confidence, a more manly self.

'I'll take it', he had said to her.

She had smiled and said nothing more. It had not been his most expensive suit purchase, though expensive enough. But it probably was his best clothing purchase.

He chose the shirt with the fine light blue stripe. And now he stood before his full length mirror, his Church's brogues polished to a fine shine, and took a long look at himself in the glass.

'I look taller in this suit. And he pulled himself up to his full six feet, thrusting back his shoulders which the tailor silently encouraged through the magic of his creation.

'No one else will wear such a suit', he expressed his thought aloud with pride. 'It is . . . a bit off the regular fare, very un-Saville Row.'

And while the thought of failing to blend in with the right people, a main reason for Athiny's adoration of the Tudor Court invitation, struck an odd note somewhere within, the thought was quickly deflected by his strong desire to wear the suit.

'I look very handsome in this suit, and more manly.' And his vanity won out.

That evening Athiny noticed five of the other men taking note of his suit. Five out of the seven other men in attendance had noticed that Athiny stood out. I am sure it is because I look very well indeed. And these, as he digested it, are men of distinction. One of them, Charles Leithe, a king of finance in the City, asked the name of his tailor. I am sure that the women, other than perhaps Mrs Weatherby, who is older and too devoted to her husband, think me very handsome indeed. I chose just the right attire for the evening, and certainly the right suit.

Whenever he caught sight of one of the women looking at him his rather petulant mouth turned up and a smirk of a smile appeared.

Dinner was served. Athiny was seated by Camille Sesemeny, a beautiful widow, probably in her early forties he guessed. Her husband was reputed to have been with MI6. And from what Athiny knew, though no one ever directly spoke about his death, a few people had mentioned China. They exchanged small talk as the servants offered them soup and salad. She had four children and when she learned that he had none the conversation flagged. Then it happened. A spot of soup dripped upon the lapel of his jacket.

Athiny wanted to excuse himself immediately to see if he could quickly remove the spot with cold water. However they had just begun dinner and it felt most inappropriate to leave the table. Athiny shifted uncomfortably in his chair. To sit with soiled attire caused him anxiety. He became self conscious. Herbert Gainsberg, seated at one head of the table and to his left, spoke to him, 'We've not met before. Tell me something of yourself Athiny', Gainsberg stated straightforwardly.

The directness of Gainsberg's approach caught Athiny off guard and momentarily removed him from his discomfort and concern for his appearance. Then he recalled that Gainsberg, while living in England for many years, was American and the directness now seemed less out of sorts.

'What would you like to know?', Athiny responded.

'What do you do? Do you work? You look rather', Gainsberg paused and took another look at Athiny. Athiny was sure that his eye alighted on that dammed spot. ' . . . rather the intellectual type, an academic perhaps?', Gainsberg asked.

'No, I've not been part of the intellectual or the academic set. I did write for a time for Culture, the British magazine on old British manor houses, their architecture, gardens, restorations, and furniture. That is where I met Elizabeth', Athiny finished.

'Oh yes. And now?', replied Gainsberg.

He won't let up Athiny said to himself. And at this point he didn't care what Gainsberg thought of the spot on his jacket lapel, he wanted to be done with him.

'Oh you know, the odd business venture, here and there.' He vastly exaggerated the truth. For his only ventures, if you could call it business, was submitting an article every so often, and less and less often in reality, to an American publication. They'd request his input on a British cultural nuance; the best way to grow roses, or how to give your new construction the appearance of the great British manor houses.

Now he was observing Gainsberg, a rather paunchy middle aged pseudo Brit, who obviously had no taste in clothes. Athiny surreptiously hazarded a glance at the man's shoes. They were old brogues, not Church's, and in desperate need of a good polishing. His hair was also in need of attention. It was too long and should have seen a barber two weeks prior. He needed a new barber for his large head and round face required the expertise of an artist to make for a becoming cut. Yes, undoubtedly, Gainsberg cared nothing for his appearance. He was probably completely unaware that he was something of a mess and would think it a great time waster to concern oneself with clothes and appearances.

'I just bought a new property', Gainsberg proferred, with the excitement of a little boy with a new bicycle. 'It's land, with a small gatehouse', he added.

'A gatehouse?', Athiny responded automatically, still contemplating his neighbour's appearance and not really listening.

'Yes. Apparently it back's onto what was the Queen Mum's property, now owned by some other royal.'

Athiny sat up. He was listening now. But Gainsberg had stopped talking and was applying himself to his food. A servant had just delivered the main course. Athiny decided he'd have to coax Gainsberg back into the conversation and get him to reveal more of with whom he was now associating.

'How did you come to this particular property?', Athiny asked with only the slightest cover to his social curiosity.

'The property was formerly owned by a Lebanese acquaintance. There are a few of them there in Cirencester', he went back to his meat.

Cirencester, quick who do I know, Athiny asked himself, in Cirencester, other than my barber. And not a single soul came to mind.

'Did I hear you say you bought that property Herbert?', Elizabeth asked from her seat at the other head of table.

Elizabeth always seems to know all that is going on at her table Athiny said to himself admiringly.

'Yes, I did', he said beaming down the table at his hostess. 'You know it's really because of you that I even had a chance to bid on the property', Gainsberg said.

Elizabeth smiled at Athiny who was unable to contain his eager curiosity which showed in his wide eyes and open mouth.

'A few years ago I'd been invited to the inauguration of a polo field there', Elizabeth said, for Athiny's benefit. 'Prior to the match a cousin of a long time family friend toured me around his gatehouse which backed onto the Queen Mum's property. He paused in his tour in front of a wall of photographs. As I stood there I realised that while I had just met this man I recognised many of the people in the photos in which he also appeared, the King of Jordan, the Sultan of Oman, that sort of thing', Elizabeth said to Athiny with laughter in her voice. 'It's probably because while I thought it rather fun I wasn't particularly impressed with all the connexions, who included the owner of the polo team, that I was introduced about.' Elizabeth, enjoying fulfilling her duty as a hostess by feeding Athiny's hunger for social tidbits, continued. 'The owner of the polo team also owned the polo field, and a rather spectacular mansion to which we were invited after the polo game. We were given scrumptious hors d'oeuvres and superb wine and later dinner. It was I think because I wasn't interested in all the connexions that he invited me to another of his parties', Elizabeth finished.

'Yes Elizabeth it was a result of my connexion with you that I could purchase that property', Gainsberg said appreciatively.

'Oh I don't know. You are well appreciated in business circles', Elizabeth said generously.

Gainsberg let out a loud laugh, 'It has nothing to do with business. Other than having the money to pay for the asking price it has to do with social connexions. Which, by the way, is exactly why that fellow who owned the gatehouse showed you his wall of photographs.'

Everyone laughed now, except Athiny. I misjudged Gainsberg, he thought to himself. Athiny felt deflated. Unconsciously his eye roved to his lapel. He couldn't get a good look at the spot without pulling his jacket out to the side at a contorted angle. So there was nothing to be done. This paunchy, poorly dressed, at least taste wise, somewhat crass fellow has managed to climb socially a fleet of rungs in one fell swoop. And climb in exalted circles. How does that happen? That should be me, backing onto the royal's property. I probably even have the money for it. If Gainsberg gained the connexion through Elizabeth so could have I. But, I didn't. He pouted. But he swiftly corrected himself, and purposefully, falsely, moved his mouth into a semi smile. Wrinkles would not do.

Athiny inwardly cringed and imperceptibly shifted right and away from Gainsberg. His shift, misunderstood by Athiny, was motivated by envy. Athiny's thoughts ran on, this boorish fellow, who has no regard for his appearance, or really for his manners either, had sailed ahead of Athiny in all social standing that counted. With the acquisition of this property he would now be in contact with the social elite. They would be nice to him, and they would invite him at some point, if he watched his 'p's' and 'q's', to a party. They would do the neighbourly thing. And unless he made a huge faux pas he'd ever after be on the right list for future invitations. Athiny wondered if Gainsberg even cared! He didn't care about his appearance, Athiny kept saying to himself. And maybe that was it. It didn't really matter to him. He was wholly indifferent as to whether he was invited or not and that made him a comfortable guest. He wouldn't fawn. They could count on his type to meld in and maybe they would find his presence or even his conversation refreshing.

How could Athiny compete with this? Compete? What was he thinking? What an uncouth word. What a disagreeable thought. And as Athiny toyed with his dessert he stole a glance sideways to see his neighbour again. Gainsberg was thoroughly enjoying his chocolate mousse. Athiny didn't want to compete with anyone let alone this boor. No, in truth Gainsberg was not a boor. He was however annoying. And I'm annoyed, he said to himself, because I would fit right in with the royals. In fact, some of them could learn a thing or two from me about good taste in clothes.

The servant came to remove the dessert plates. Athiny noticed his dessert remained mostly uneaten while it looked like Gainsberg had licked his plate clean! I can't stand it. And now they're all moving into the drawing room chatting and laughing. And that social snob, Anthony Berkeley, isn't he related to that historic Bishop Berkeley, has moved in on Gainsberg. He wants to learn no doubt exactly where Gainsberg's new property is so he can casually pop by in hopes of hob knobbing with, probably Lady Kenning. Isn't she recently widowed? All these thoughts churned in Athiny's mind as he moved mechanically along with the others out of the dining room.

I don't feel up to it. I don't want to sit in the drawing room listening to Berkeley dropping names nor Gainsburger, I mean Gainsberg, gleefully anticipating his climb as he becomes acquainted with his new neighbours. I can't stomach it. Suddenly Athiny looked about for his hostess.

'Elizabeth, what a lovely dinner', he tried to smile.

'I'm glad you enjoyed it', she moved in his direction.

She really is charming, and her hair falls beautifully around her face, always cut to accentuate her lovely bone structure. And her gown hangs perfectly and just the right teal blue for her colouring, Athiny said inwardly.

'I'm afraid however I must leave early. I'm so sorry. I've not been getting enough sleep and tomorrow is my riding day. You will forgive me?'

'Of course. I'm happy you could come. And I hope you'll join us again soon. Give that beautiful bay mare of yours a good pat for me', she said with genuine enthusiasm.

She exudes life and charm he said to himself. And to Elizabeth he said, 'I will. Belmare will appreciate your affection', and he kissed her hand.

She walked with him to the entrance where Chalmers was ready at the door.

'Goodnight', said Elizabeth and she waved Athiny down the drive as he walked to where his car was parked.

'Goodnight', he replied.

And as he drove home he considered the best way to remove the spot of soup from his jacket lapel. It would have been much easier if he could have immediately applied cold water. Now it would require more than mere cold water which two hours ago would have sufficed. With not another thought for anyone at the party he zoomed down the empty road thinking of his large laundry sink and saving his suit.

CHAPTER SEVEN

THE CASE OF PRIDE

'You look particularly pleased Miss Elizabeth', Morris, Elizabeth's housekeeper, said as Elizabeth came to the luncheon table to check arrangements.

'I am, Morris. Clarity is coming today. Do you remember Clarity Freeman? She was here in the Fall', Elizabeth spoke rapidly as she glided around the table checking arrangements, adjusting a vase, and flattening the table cloth at a corner.

'Yes I do Mamam. Miss Freeman is brimming with life', replied Morris.

Elizabeth laughed, 'Isn't she though. Thank you Morris everything looks lovely. The flowers are beautiful. Did George pick these for you this morning?'

'Yes he did. George knows that you enjoy stock, he has been cultivating all the colours for you', Morris said.

'How good of him. He has done a fine job', Elizabeth responded, smiling. She lightly patted Morris's arm as they left the room. Elizabeth moved swiftly up the stairs to change for the luncheon.

'If anyone arrives before I'm down have Chalmers seat them in the parlour', she called over her shoulder.

'Yes Mamam', Morris responded.

The door knocker resounded in the entryway of Tudor Court. Chalmers, expecting Elizabeth's guests for luncheon, opened wide the large old oak door.

'Chalmers', Samuel Estheren smiled, 'We've come at Miss Fennington's invitation for luncheon.'

Chalmers, recognising Mr Estheren and his two companions Miss Beveridge and Mr William Wyman, and fully aware of his employer's plans for the day's luncheon, stepped back to let them enter.

'Would you kindly wait in the parlour?', Chalmers said. 'Miss Fennington is expecting you.'

'Thank you Chalmers. I know where it is', Estheren replied with a touch of pride, displaying to his companions that he had been to Tudor Court perhaps more often than had they.

Five minutes later Chalmers was again called to the door as two guests arrived. Mr and Mrs Everett Weatherby, a charming older couple whom Chalmers secretly liked very much, announced themselves.

'Please come in', Chalmers even smiled as he greeted them, an expression normally absent to guests, who were regularly treated with a stiff upper lip.

'Miss Fennington should be down any moment now', he added. 'May I bring you to the parlour?'

Chalmers, walking a little more slowly than his normal clip for the Weatherby's, opened the parlour doors, letting them pass in ahead. Then, standing in the entryway Chalmers announced,

'Mr and Mrs Everett Weatherby.' Chalmers left the room and closed the doors behind him.

As Chalmers returned to the main hallway Elizabeth was descending the stairs from the upper rooms.

'Did I hear voices Chalmers?', she asked.

'Yes Mamam. Mr Estheren arrived with Miss Beveridge and Mr Wyman. The Weatherby's followed. They are in the parlour together.'

'Very good. That leaves Pedigree and Clarity. I hope Clarity arrives last that I may bring her in myself', Elizabeth said.

'Mamam is looking forward to seeing Miss Freeman again', Chalmers said, having noted the twinkle in his mistress's eye.

Elizabeth laughed, 'Yes I am. Clarity is a breath of fresh air. And offers a good example for being oneself, all forms of posturing absent. Do you think a few of my guests might benefit from such an example?', she asked, her eyes twinkling back at him.

Chalmers, smiling ever so slightly, nodded sagaciously. The door knocker resounded. A moment later Paulus Pedigree was ushered in.

The moment Pedigree saw Elizabeth standing in the hall the placid contentment of his face melted into a smile.

'Hello Paulus. You are very well I hope', Elizabeth said graciously.

'Yes thank you. And you must be. You look very well indeed', he replied, warming to Elizabeth's company.

'I am, thank you. Would you join our guests in the parlour? Chalmers will show you. I'm waiting for Clarity Freeman. As she is coming alone I want to bring her in myself', Elizabeth added.

'Of course', replied Pedigree.

Pedigree handed Chalmers his hat and stepped firmly ahead of the butler toward the parlour, his nose in the air. Chalmers winked at Elizabeth. Elizabeth stifled a laugh. Chalmers had been her grandfather's butler in the latter years and to her recollection she had seen him wink but once before.

Elizabeth opened the old oak door in anticipation of her visitor. A glorious summer day greeted her. The birds sang and all the colour of life was highlighted in warm sunlight. And there coming up the drive was Clarity's little old Alfa Romeo. Elizabeth skipped down the front steps and tripped along the drive to where Clarity was parking her car. Clarity jumped out of her car and the two friends warmly embraced.

Clarity, laughing, exuded, 'You look wonderful. How very good to see you.'

'And you!', Elizabeth's smile shone, 'I'm so happy to see you. So happy that you are here', emphasizing the last word.

Answering her friend's unspoken question Clarity replied, 'Yes you're right I've just come from Africa. Roger Balerer comes down to help an arm of his charity in Ethiopia. His foundation is helping educate children and I was doing some teaching. You know, my Socratic style, open up yourself and mind to learning', Clarity was beaming as she spoke.

'Yes, I know my dear, you're such a boon to all who cross your path', Elizabeth said with genuine enthusiasm. 'Did you get in a dialogue with Roger? I love watching him play tennis.'

'Yes, sort of. He came and sat in on one of the dialogues with the children. Afterward he asked me about it. He's quite astute. He'd noticed a few young faces lighting up, awakening to the importance of thinking about who one chooses to be in life, character wise', she smiled.

'Oh that's wonderful', Elizabeth said, squeezing her friend's hand. They laughed together as arm in arm they walked up the drive to the house. An especially bright glow of sunshine lit their figures and seemed to reflect from them as they walked together.

Once all were settled in the dining room, Mrs Weatherby said, 'We were in Africa dear, in Kenya. I loved the giraffe, so graceful. It was wonderful to see them run. But, well, it is not as it is here, of course it's not. But I mean you can't just ring up a neighbour or friend and go for tea', she finished with a little furrow in her brow.

They had just enjoyed a split pea and bean soup and were now served salmon, asparagus, and salad. Mrs Weatherby was seated by her husband and Mr Wyman, and she spoke across the table to Clarity.

'Yes I know what you mean', responded Clarity brightly. 'I would have liked to have seen more of the animals in the wild. I spend a lot of time with the children and they are my great delight. The young Ethiopian children are happy, eager to learn, and open to strangers. I think they respond particularly to someone new because they find a lot of fun in someone different from themselves.'

Mrs Weatherby was listening and her husband was nodding. Mr Weatherby said, 'Yes I think that is right. African children are more interested in that which is different from themselves than are British children', he looked pensive.

Mr Wyman spoke, 'When we volunteered in our local school I noticed the children were interested in a newcomer momentarily, almost as a curiosity. But the interest died quickly and they withdrew back to their own favoured and familiar company.'

Mr Estheren and Miss Beveridge were in their own conversation speaking quietly together. Paulus Pedigree was observing and listening to Clarity.

'Of course they would delight in you Clarity', Elizabeth said with warmth. 'You are real. And children always respond with fervour to the genuine article.'

Mr Weatherby smiled. And Pedigree felt Weatherby's simple response to Elizabeth's and Clarity's honest and invigorating sense of life. Why have I nothing to add, Pedigree asked himself. Normally I would jump in when Elizabeth spoke, and respond to her interest with interest. He slowly ate his meal.

Pedigree realised he'd been observing Elizabeth and Clarity engaging with each other. One could not help notice their unusual energy for life. They were laughing together again. He'd missed the transition from the topic of the children and didn't know of what they were now speaking. What was it about Clarity? 'Children always respond to the genuine article',

Elizabeth had said. That was it. Clarity was genuine. Genuine. What does that really mean? Pedigree looked across at Weatherby. He was happily engaged with his wife. They were enjoying their meal, happy to be together and in this company. Pedigree suddenly felt alone. But I'm always alone, he thought. I like directing my own time, unencumbered. But I've not felt alone before.

Pedigree picked up his wine glass and glanced over again at Weatherby. Yes, the man was genuinely happy. Pedigree heard a snippet of the conversation. Something about Africa and how perhaps they should go again. He looked more intently at Mrs Weatherby's face. Her expression betrayed an adoring affection for her husband. They were happy. He looked again at Elizabeth and Clarity in conversation together. And suddenly Pedigree realised that between this elderly couple and these two genuine friends there was a real contrast with the others with whom he consumed his time. Something dawned upon him. Those with whom I deal, socialize, all with whom I associate, and perhaps all in fact whom I know, speak without openness. They have an angle from which they come, an objective toward which they are moving. How can this include any happiness? In conversation with them one is part of the objective. In association one is a witting dupe to their usage, to their advancement. Of course, one was supposed to be advancing oneself in the same way. But where was the meaning? Where was friendship in all of this? There could be no true friendship with such people. Paulus Pedigree felt his shoulders sag, he felt cold inside. He'd always thought he had many friends. And they were rich, and beautiful.

They lived in beautiful homes, travelled, and were cultured. But in this moment he knew they were not friends.

Without openness, where was the honesty, the truth? Truth was not merely withheld, or hidden through the choice of not being open. The cunning practise of not naming the question, or of speaking around the question meant not being able to find the truth, of losing the path to the truth. Over time, truth lost, withheld, unspoken, became unrecognisable.

Now after seventy years Pedigree did not wish to face this moment. For here was the heretofore unknown truth. In losing the truth he had also lost he knew not what in all these years. He had not recognised all this time that his interest and his life energy had gone in the wrong direction, had gone for nought. While he could still recognise this truth, he could not face the change from within that it called forth. For to make a change in the very frame of mind from which he lived would be a full open acknowledgement that he had been wrong. That he, Paulus Pedigree, had chosen the wrong way of leading his life. He paused as all this now dawned upon him. Had he in fact led his life? Or had he followed what he had foolishly admired without thinking?

He swallowed, barely able to continue now with this line of thought. He had admired money, the chic clique. He admired his cousin Vernon Athiny, always so perfectly dressed and mannered. He'd admired the surface without bothering to look for the substance. And so the truth was he had not led his life. He'd allowed himself, his life, to be led by the influences around him instead of deciding what was the best life to live. He'd been proud of his associations, always invited to the parties of the rich, the powerful, always included whenever and wherever the intelligentsia were. Instead of stopping and thinking about what was most important, he'd let time lead him to his deserved outcome. And so his life had gone. And life was almost gone. Seventy years without stopping to truly reflect. This young woman, Clarity Freeman, had shown him with her open genuine love of life, in two hours, who he had become. Was she even thirty? He shivered inside with shame.

But now that I can see who I am, now that I have actually gained clarity for the truth, I cannot make the change. He looked down at the linen napkin in his lap, not wanting to raise his head in case Clarity or Elizabeth should look his way. Suddenly something else dawned on him. In an instant it came to him that Elizabeth was very much like Clarity. He heard the two women laughing together again. In spite of himself he glanced up and saw their faces. They were alight with life. The sun from the window was shining upon the table and seemed to alight on them especially. The beams seemed to be drawn to their faces, expressions of happy life. There was a secret there, they held it between them. Yet it was there for anyone to see, if one wanted to see. It was an open unafraid bold seizing of life. An understanding that life is to be lived and to live it one must be true, true to oneself and true to life. The moment with the sunbeams on their faces seemed a highlighting from the heavens, a just recognition for deep appreciation of life. And the appreciation was the key in the present to an earned happiness and future. Why hadn't I seen it before? I have been coming to

Fennington parties for almost twenty years. And the others who come now to Elizabeth's parties are like I am, interested in furthering themselves. The words came slowly to his mind. He spoke them slowly in his head. Elizabeth often had a visitor, as Clarity was visiting today, an outsider really. As I think about it it is an outsider who can be the mirror to oneself. I never wanted to be an outsider. No it is too hard. I cannot face that mirror, he cried alone to himself. I have always wanted to fit in, to fit in with the important people, the accomplished, the achievers, the educated, the moneyed.

Paulus pondered this realisation. It would take an outsider to show me who I am. To change my life, my friends, to change my mind about what is important, now that would be something. The change would require a complete turnaround of my entire perspective on life. It would mean addressing and living for what matters. And it would mean turning from looking at the wrong things to seeking to do the right thing with my life. He spoke very slowly to himself now. He knew he had to listen to the truth.

Blindly he accepted the dessert the maid offered him. He was unaware of the moments and minutes that passed. He was unaware of the conversation around him. He had been struck by this revelation, stopped in his tracks. Now he was grappling with what this young vibrant woman at Elizabeth's table was showing him, that which he had been so unwilling to see. It was right in front of him now. None of what he had placed store in, of what he thought he valued, had any value. Seventy years. He cringed within.

His wine glass was empty. He hadn't noticed that he'd drunk all his wine. The others were getting up from the table. Elizabeth was looking at him.

'Is everything alright?', she asked.

He got up from the table and looked at her with a new realisation. Elizabeth wasn't one of us. And he cringed inwardly again at his self realisation.

He was finally able to speak, 'Thank you. I'm fine. I . . . was thinking about your visitor, Clarity. She is . . . she has a different perspective.' He stopped. Elizabeth was listening attentively and a slight smile appeared upon her lips. She nodded, and waited. Pedigree kept looking at Elizabeth.

There was a silence, and then she said, 'Would you like to join us in the garden?'

For the first time since he could remember, it must be years, decades, he wasn't sure what he wanted. Nothing he wanted he valued now. Normally he would join the party without question. But now he was hesitating. Elizabeth waited.

'I think I'll use your bathroom for a moment,' he was able to say.

'Of course', she said, still looking at him. She smiled and turned to go and join her other guests.

He moved almost unconsciously toward the hall from where he could find the bathroom. Pedigree felt at sea. He got to the hall. Then, down the hall a ways, to the left he found the door to the bathroom. He opened the door. Then he found the light switch. He switched it on. He entered the bathroom, closed the door behind him, and locked it. He faced himself in the mirror.

Suddenly he said to the self in the mirror, 'I don't know you. I don't know myself.'

He stared at the mirror. Then he whispered, 'Is it that I never did know myself?' He waited. He stared at the seventy year old image that faced him. Then he said to the image, asking, 'And . . . now . . . I'm getting a glimpse?'

Paulus flashed over his life. He had worked. He had risen in the corporate environs of Hughes and Henry, one of the largest consumer packaged goods firms worldwide. And he had been proud of his achievement, proud of himself. He had surpassed many along the road to those executive offices on the top floor. Even now he smiled to himself as he recalled all he'd done. I knew how to get things done, to get others to get things done for me, for the team. And he imagined himself walking those hallowed halls of the eighty eighth floor. He stopped smiling. He remembered how hurt, crushed, and angry, he'd been when H&H did not offer him that top position of Senior Vice President worldwide. Those hallowed halls held snobs. While they promised reward for merit, they had withheld it from him. For they had also held an invisible code, holding choice positions for the kind, the class, that fit in. And they had judged that he did not fit. Paulus had resented this, he still resented this, deeply. He had not been able to strain to consider that perhaps the cause of the failure and this unhappiness, lay not in others but within himself, in his failure to recognise the truth.

He had quit. He had left those hallowed halls telling himself that they, all those snobs, behind all those doors, didn't deserve him. That was all he could tell himself at the time. Because up until then he'd considered himself one of them. One of the elite. Now the elite were snobs, arrogant posturing snobs underserving of his company and capabilities. And somehow there was a discrepancy, a non-sequitur, a big question as to whether he had been one of them all along. And a bigger question yet, who wastes life by holding the wrong values and thus pursuing the wrong course? He could not face this question. Nor, could he face what the question might mean. For pride is friend to fear.

Pride. Paulus knew it was pride that held him and that had him hold onto the hurt all this time. It was pride that kept him from going elsewhere, and more importantly, from going elsewhere in his thinking, just as it was pride that kept him from seeing the truth. Now he knew that it was his pride that kept him from facing himself. And he could see something else. There was a laziness of mind, of thinking. Not an inability. Rather, a laziness that he had allowed. It was far easier to deal with oneself if when your mind turned to the truth, turned to what you didn't want to see about yourself, your motives, or what you truly thought of yourself, you turned away. One turned away from the truth for fear of what one might find. Fear of puncturing one's pride and having to pick up one's deflated ego off the floor was unbearable to consider. One allowed this turning from the truth because if given permission, one's thinking would uncover that laziness, dig it out. And in the uprooting, discover what had been lost as a result of sloth in thinking. And the next step would be to answer the question, why did I allow such laziness? Who permits such sloth? And, what is to be done about it? A remedy would need be found for the years of neglect. And it wasn't even all the work that concerned him. It was the recognition required, the acknowledgement of fault, the great error in failing to reflect along the way, the actual speaking aloud to the laziness, naming it, that had stopped him from facing the truth. Pride.

What had he missed seeing? How had his vision, his thinking, been clouded? And there is something else. It is most frightening to go after a dream full bore which requires dealing with all the barriers, like pride, that are in one's way. Far better, as guarantee for the ego, to find an excuse for missing the mark for a better life and for being happier. So he had allowed for an excuse, another kind of laziness. Even a never spoken excuse (I didn't stop to think, I placed too much importance on what other people think, I had four children and if I'd not I would have adventured), was still an excuse. These were excuses, but the truth is different. The truth is more often that one wanted money, power, and position because it is what other people value. Other people can understand money, power, and position. He had wanted others' recognition, he had wanted to be liked. It had been more important to fit in, than to know himself. And the consequence was that he could not know himself. He had permitted pride to get in the way. He had let pride break the relationship with himself. Could life be wasted any more than through pride? There was that word that once he had ignored or on occasion when allowed to enter his purview had felt satisfying, and that now stung. Stinging, he stopped.

He changed the subject on himself. He asked himself, 'Shall I join them?' And he didn't know the answer. 'Do I want to join them?', he tried again. 'I don't know', he said a little more firmly. 'I don't know?', he asked. 'How can that be? I've always known.' He sat down on the toilet seat. Something about the clarity of that girl, her fresh faced, open hearted character caught me. She has caught my conscious. And now I'm stuck. I'm stuck in some netherland between what I know, or knew, and what can be. 'Can it be?', he asked himself. He whispered softly 'Can I be', he hesitated, 'myself?', and he knew not to whom he asked the question. He shook his head. He shook his body, trying, to shake himself, to wake himself.

'No. It is too hard. I cannot face that mirror', he cried to himself, alone. His head dropped and he placed his head in his hands. His thoughts were completely new to him. There is another life. Another life. There is another way of living that I did not know existed. Clarity lives it. And, in the next moment he said, 'Elizabeth lives it.' Why haven't I seen this? I've been coming here for twenty years. That's how long I've known Elizabeth. But I haven't known her. He raised his head from his hands in bewildered surprise. 'I don't understand', he said aloud. How could I have not seen this. Not only do Elizabeth and Clarity share so much that is of importance, they are living this . . . other life.

What is it? His mind recalled the ringing laughter between Elizabeth and Clarity he'd heard at the luncheon table. Their laughter was full of life, their conversation was one that sources in openness, appreciation, and splashes out in exuberance. They were simply being themselves. And morsels of knowledge came as bullets to his pride. Elizabeth and Clarity were wholly unconcerned with making impressions. They were deeply comfortable in their own skin. They know who they are. And his head dropped again into his hands. Seventy years. Seventy years, and I don't know myself. Then another thought arrived. Did Elizabeth know what she was doing? He sat up. Had she brought all of us together to learn? In another moment he stood up. He shivered at his inclusion in the group of which he had long been so proud to be a part, about which he now felt so differently. For a moment his disconsolateness left him and he felt a momentary exhilaration, a thrilling feeling of possible revelation. Had Elizabeth planned this? Was this, Tudor Court, where many ambitious and powerful people met to further their positions, status, and sense of pride, a plan for a purpose quite different than for what guests assumed they came?

His mind went back to Elizabeth's face as he had seen her while they both stood by the luncheon table. She had been looking intently at him. And a slight smile had crossed her lips. Yes, she had recognised his confusion. Had she also recognised the realisation that now had him in its grasp? Now that he realised these two wholly different types of lives he could see two worlds and their boundaries. One had a fence of pride, the other was unbordered, without limits. The question arrived. Do I have the courage to acknowledge that I've been living a pseudo life? Do I have the courage to begin to live anew, to live a full life? Do

I have the courage to be? To be myself? To be fully alive to this life? To be or not to be. Shakespeare figured it out four hundred years ago. For that is the question, because that must be how one is truly alive, by being who one has been given to be.

He felt weak inside. He sensed that he could easily shrink from this responsibility. Yes. That is what he now recognised as the truth. This life is a personal responsibility. It is not merely my own, as my possessions are, to do with as I may. No. While I may have earned my possessions, I did not earn this gift. And he placed his hand on his chest over his heart. He felt a deep sadness at his loss, lost time. Lost life. And in the next moment tears of joy came to his eyes as in that instant he felt a deep gratitude for life. I may be seventy but I am still alive. He turned to the mirror again. This time he was unafraid to face his reflection. He stood. He looked into his own eyes. And instead of an image, he saw himself. He straightened his shoulders, and stood taller. I will join them in the garden he said to himself. And Pedigree walked out of the bathroom, into the hall, and down the hallway toward the outdoors and the garden.

CHAPTER EIGHT

THE CASE OF PRIDE UNDONE

Paulus reached the garden gate and hesitated. He heard a murmur of voices further into the garden, then opening the gate he stepped into the garden. In the moment of closing the gate behind him he felt a closing of a chapter, a very long chapter of his life. A ring of happy laughter met his ears. 'Elizabeth and Clarity', he whispered, and smiled. And he moved toward that clear warm welcoming ring of life.

'Paulus', Elizabeth called. Elizabeth had seen him before he had seen the group, recognising a change in his demeanour, intuitively she had called to him.

Paulus walked slowly but directly toward the group to join them and inadvertently he took a deep breath. Noticing the clean fresh air of the garden, and too the scent of roses, another small smile appeared on his face.

'Isn't it lovely? There is nothing quite like the air of a thriving garden', said Clarity. And her words were words of understanding and welcome. Without thinking about it Paulus moved toward Clarity and seated himself beside her on the bench.

'Do you have a garden Mr Pedigree?', asked Mrs Weatherby.

'Oh please call me Paulus', he said. He had liked hearing his first name, something inside was warming to the feeling of hearing it spoken.

'Yes, yes I do have a garden', Paulus responded. He paused. 'I haven't put much effort into it I have to admit', he was surprised to hear himself say this. For he had taken pride in how his gardener kept his garden.

'It is so beautiful here', he said to Mrs Weatherby, realising that he was taking in his surroundings in the moment, 'that I must have a good conversation with Rufus my gardener and learn more of his ideas and what we might grow in the garden', he finished.

Mrs Weatherby smiled, 'Oh good. It's such a pleasure, a true enjoyment, being in and working in one's garden'. Paulus heard her childlike enthusiasm. 'I think you'll find it a great way to relax, and reflect too', she added.

'Thank you', Paulus returned, slowly taking in and appreciating her meaning.

'What do you recommend for a new garden enthusiast?', Elizabeth asked Mrs Weatherby, on Paulus's behalf.

'Well, I think it is important to know what you like. Which flowers, trees, bushes, shrubs, plants, appeal to you? Is scent important to you, and if so what fragrances? Is it colour you're after? Do you like an orderly feel to things? Or, do you prefer something more wild feeling?', Mrs Weatherby looked at Clarity when she said this. And Clarity caught her eye, and in that moment the two laughed together.

Paulus was listening to Mrs Weatherby bubbling over. And when the older woman and the younger woman laughed simultaneously in a moment they shared he caught himself with his mouth open and laughed too. All heads turned to this new sound, Paulus's laugh. Paulus blushed, and then everyone laughed together, even Paulus, who was now laughing at himself for the first time in his life.

Paulus drove home slowly. A heightened awareness had come upon him. It was as a visitation had caused another state of being for it affected him completely. And the overall effect was a desire to notice, to see, all around him. There was a yearning too, a longing, to understand the connections in life to more and more life. It was the meaning he sought. He wanted to know the meaning of things he'd never even noticed before in all his seventy years.

'I think I'm beginning to understand the meaning of the sound in Clarity's and Elizabeth's laughter. That was the first thing that struck me this day. Even before the visitation.' This was the name Paulus was giving to the cause of his new state.

'And the visitation first joined me in the bathroom. It was hoovering there, waiting for me to recognise and to face myself in that mirror. I had to face my reflection. I had to be willing to reflect on the whole picture, on my life, before the visitation would alight on me. And, then . . .' and he smiled, and not a small smile, 'it came to me. It's funny to name it 'it'. For it feels warm, real, alive, within me now', Paulus paused reflecting.

'He', Paulus started in again, 'yes that is better, he is as a friend.' And Paulus sat up straight, quite straight in the seat of his car. 'Look', he exclaimed to himself, to life, 'just look at the green of all the bushes. And the trees. Beautiful', and he felt the sunlight reaching for him, warming him in his car. He was noticing his drive home, he was seeing anew the route he had known, but not truly known, not appreciated, all these years.

Paulus drove up the short gravel drive to his house and stopped a little way off from where he normally parked his car. He held onto the steering wheel and bent down low to peer over it at his house. He switched off the ignition. He looked for a full five minutes, taking in the house in its setting of trees and bushes.

'It's quite a nice house', Paulus said aloud. And hearing himself he laughed. 'Yes, I quite like my house.' And he laughed again. 'It's not too large, not too small. I've always liked that mottled green I chose years ago. And that deep, tarnished burgundy for the window frames, it works very well.'

Paulus opened the car door and stepped out. He stood there breathing in the clean air. 'How wonderful, the country air is. All the plant life, all the oxygen the plants provide, clean air.' And Paulus turned slowly in a circle, still standing on the packed gravel, to see and take in the setting of his house.

'I love the simplicity, the simple setting of the house flanked by the enormous trees and with bushes along the sides of the path up to the house. The house is placed beautifully in nature. Simplicity is something I've always known to be of great value.' And Paulus was pleased, he took a simple pride, the right kind of pride, in the knowledge that allowed him now to appreciate the gift he had before him.

'I haven't properly appreciated my property before.' And this recognition humbled him.

He moved away from his car and began to walk. He strolled in order to take in the detail of where he lived. Rufus had been planting. He had planted purple petunias along the little gravel path that led from the drive along to the side of the house.

'They are lovely', and Paulus stooped down low to catch their fragrance. 'Oh', he exclaimed, as he caught the scent of a group of purple petunias. He got down on his knees and put his nose right into the thick of a patch of purple. And Paulus took a number of breaths enjoying their scent, a scent he liked very much he decided.

And he laughed, 'Ohh, I had not appreciated this fragrance. I like it very much.' And then he said, 'I must thank Rufus for choosing these lovely flowers.' He had been talking aloud to himself since he first got in his car to drive home from Tudor Court.

Paulus stood, and stayed standing sensing something important had just occurred. It was in the kneeling. What was it? It was as a ghost across the stage. He waited. Please, he called out from within. What was the ghost? In asking, in seeking the beauty in the scent of the flower I knelt and the kneeling is humbling and in being humbled one can begin to deal directly with pride.

Paulus walked on, touching a thick trunked tree as he passed. He stopped and placed the palm of his hand on its bark and thinking as he did all the years it had lived here. Paulus's smile broadened. He had been smiling since stopping the car to properly appreciate his house. He continued toward the house.

'The green grass is a lush green, some of the leaves are new and a light fresh green. Oh how beautiful.' And he stopped again. He stood, taking in the house from his new perspective, taking in the very moment itself. 'I love it. I love the beauty of the setting, the scent of the earth, of plant life growing, the greens, the clean air, and I love that I live here.' Appreciating and looking at the house anew he felt something else. It was something entirely new. He stood, looking at his house, waiting. Then slowly it came, 'This house, my house, . . .' it was there, he was just about to grasp it, 'it . . . could be . . . a home. A home', Paulus let the words wing themselves in the open air to where his eyes were set on the green and burgundy and stone structure. 'A home', Paulus repeated. 'How?', he asked. And he let the question wing its way, beyond the house, to where it was to go.

CHAPTER NINE

FRIENDS AT TUDOR COURT

Clarity could stay for three days. Then she would return to Ethiopia and her work there for another three months. In the meantime Elizabeth had invited her to visit. They had visited together at Tudor Court before. Neither suggested plans for their time together, both knowing the time would unfold naturally, enjoyably.

'That was a lovely luncheon Elizabeth', Clarity said after the guests had left.

'I think everyone enjoyed themselves', Elizabeth replied. 'I wasn't sure Paulus would rejoin us. I was happy that he did', she added.

'Yes', Clarity paused in thought. 'He was very pleased to be able to rejoin us, and he brought a new energy and life with him. I was happy for him.'

Elizabeth smiled, 'Yes my dear, and it is that generous spirit in you that helps others find their own good spirit. He sat down right beside you.'

Clarity laughed, 'He did.' A moment passed. 'Shall we go outdoors again?', she asked.

'Yes let's', Elizabeth responded enthusiastically. 'Let's run up and change and go directly.'

Clarity was back downstairs first. Elizabeth met her a few minutes later at the main rear outside door.

'I see you made ready for our adventure', Clarity said, tapping the Wellington boot she was putting on. There by the door stood the other pair of Wellingtons for Elizabeth's use.

Elizabeth laughed, 'Morris put them here for us. He is very good at anticipating needs.'

Once outdoors Elizabeth and Clarity were in their natural element. If Wellingtons were better for running the two would have run most of the way to the stream. Clarity stooped to pick two dandelion stems that had gone to seed.

'Here's yours', she said exuberantly, handing one to Elizabeth.

'Ready?', Elizabeth responded.

'Yes!', Clarity exclaimed.

And the two, eyes closed, took a deep breath simultaneously and blew hard the fuzzy seed circle into the other's face.

The two burst out laughing. Elizabeth said, 'I hope you made a good wish.'

'I did', Clarity responded. 'And I know you did.' They ran the rest of the distance through the meadow toward the stream on the other side.

'Where are the horses?', asked Clarity, when they'd reached the edge of the meadow.

'Langley has them in the other meadow on the other side of the wood. We'll ride tomorrow if you like', Elizabeth looked to Clarity.

'Yes, let's', Clarity enthused.

In a few moments the moving water of the stream and the surrounding trees of the forest quieted the spirit. And they each felt the peace of mind and spirit they knew they would find here.

Quiet, they stood in the stream and then stepping along the stream bed, Clarity spoke, 'Thank you so much Elizabeth for having me here. I think of this very place when I'm in Africa', she paused.

'You do?', Elizabeth asked quietly.

'Yes. The cool and the quiet are great solace to the soul', she replied and stopped. Elizabeth waited, wondering what Clarity's trials were.

'The children are wonderful, and so responsive. So very appreciative of one's attentions, teaching, and of one's love. And some of them need so very much. One can do without food for a time, but one cannot do for too long without love,' she paused again. Then Clarity continued, 'Just to know that someone loves you, even if they are not there at that moment or time, is enough to carry on. Once a child is old enough to understand that one will return a young child can do well. They will commit to learning, will even try to be a better boy or girl and tend to their character if he or she knows you are coming back', Clarity finished. She had been walking downstream and Elizabeth was behind her. Elizabeth came up to be right beside Clarity. They stood side by side looking downstream for a few moments. Silently Elizabeth put her arms around Clarity, the two embraced, Clarity holding on tightly for a long time.

Clarity let go and looking at Elizabeth said through her tears, 'I can never leave them Elizabeth.'

Elizabeth, looking into her eyes recognising that the tears were tears of deep love for the children and at the same time tears of love and longing for her home and England's green land, said, 'Someone else will join you and take over for you.'

'There are others who love the children too,' Clarity said slowly. 'But the children need to know that someone will be there for them always.'

They walked out of the stream and onto the bank and sat down with their feet still in the flowing waters.

'You know I have dreamed of a man arriving to join me there,' Clarity smiled.

Elizabeth replied, 'It would be lovely to share the joy and the burden. There is someone out there who can do that. And with you', she added slowly.

Clarity turned to look at Elizabeth. Then she asked, 'Do you think so?'

'Yes I do. You are very special Clarity. And you have already worked very hard for someone so young. But there is someone like you who needs you too. Someone who will relate to you, one who will even understand you', Elizabeth finished.

'Understand', Clarity repeated the word. 'Now that would be something, something wonderful,' she smiled her full warm smile. She was quiet for a number of minutes. Then she stood up and Elizabeth stood with her. Clarity put her arm around Elizabeth this time and raised her other arm out to the place where they stood.

'What a wonderful world,' she said.

And they began to sing together, 'I see trees of green, red roses too. I see them bloom for me and you. And I think to myself, what a wonderful world. I hear a baby cry and watch him grow (and tears streamed down Clarity's face) he'll learn much more than I'll ever know and I sing to my friend (and they hugged each other) what a wonderful world.'

That evening Elizabeth and Clarity had dinner in the dining room at Tudor Court. Elizabeth thought Clarity would enjoy being served. Morris had personally laid the table for them and George had picked a posy of colourful and fragrant sweet peas and placed them in a beautiful old pottery jug off to the side and between the two settings. Mary roasted a chicken, and prepared a cranberry orange salad and a light vegetable soup. Clarity and Elizabeth had fun dressing for dinner and came down the stairs together arm in arm. Chalmers was waiting at the foot of the stairs to escort them to the dining room.

Clarity giggled, 'Oh Elizabeth what fun!' She took Chalmers arm and leaning forward indicated Elizabeth should take his other arm and as she did even Chalmers could not help but laugh, partaking in the exuberant life in his midst. The Tudor Court staff, aware of the good friendship between Elizabeth and Clarity and seeing the fun and informality that surrounded it enjoyed playing their part.

'And do you think of a man sharing your life?', Clarity asked her friend as they sat across from one another in the quiet and privacy of Tudor Court's dining room.

'I don't think of a man. Perhaps if there was a man whom I liked very much I would begin to think of him, the particular man', Elizabeth replied.

'Yes, that would be much better. If one knew someone, saw someone everyday, a colleague, a neighbour who sparked one's interest, that would be fun and interesting to consider the possibilities', Clarity said.

'Do you think it happens like that?', Elizabeth asked.

'You do not?', her friend replied.

'I mean. I think it is more likely to happen suddenly. Suddenly someone is there in front of you, at a party, on the street, a stranger. Someone you meet unexpectedly. And you know in a few minutes, I want to get to know this person', Elizabeth offered.

'Is that how it has happened for you?', Clarity asked her friend.

'Yes. Whenever I have met a man in whom I have interest it has been like that', Elizabeth replied.

'And has he known too?' Clarity continued to inquire.

'No, not necessarily. However something about my knowing registers and awakens him. Perhaps its - 'She knows something to which I need to pay more attention', Elizabeth shared in a more masculine deeper voice, and laughed.

Clarity laughed, 'Now that sounds like fun – something that would inspire desire for further discovery.'

Elizabeth replied, 'Yes it is fun. And more, I believe it is good, valuable, to know oneself well enough that you can see when and how to respond in the moment.'

'Yes indeed', her friend said. 'Also, I think the other person, privy to your keen insight, should appreciate the opportunity for discovery of your person.'

' . . . knowledge is appealing. Perhaps it is appealing because another would like to have such knowledge, knowledge of self, knowledge about life itself', Elizabeth finished.

'Are you saying that in knowing oneself one can then also know another far better than otherwise?', Clarity asked.

'Yes, that's right', Elizabeth answered.

'And how has this knowledge served you?', Clarity continued.

'I think well. My initial recognition of a potential match, at least a match of some degree, has been correct. As for a long term match I don't think one can necessarily expect that.'

'And what about a long term match? Marriage?', Clarity asked.

'Are you asking do I want that?', Elizabeth replied with a question.

'Yes', Clarity replied simply.

'I don't know', Elizabeth answered.

'You would know though if the right person appeared', Clarity asked rhetorically.

'I would know if it were the right person. However I cannot say that I know I would choose to join my life with him', Elizabeth said.

'Ah, that is interesting. It is certainly unusual, and not surprising', and she smiled at her friend.

The dinner had long been eaten when the conversation ended and they both went up to bed. Clarity stood by the huge window in her room and looked out onto the lawns and the trees where the last vestiges of light hung in light pinks on the western horizon.

'How beautiful', she said aloud. 'How lucky I am to be here and to know Elizabeth.'

She thought of how different the African skies were. The cloud shapes didn't want to become images in her imagination. I love to see the giants, monsters, and big hats in our clouds. She thought of how she loved the familiar turning of the light here. As the last of the day's light died away the stars came out. The whole of Tudor Court was enveloped in black night. It was the stars turn to shine. The night sky was alight with white dots and some were twinkling. It is a wonderful world. She thought again of their singing, of being with Elizabeth, of being at Tudor Court, she was thankful. She left the window and went to the big four poster bed without canopy. Clarity propped up the large down pillows so she could tuck in and still see out the window. She pulled the thick white cotton covered down duvet around her and sank into its soft folds.

'What a dreamy sky', she said aloud. 'All those stars, all that distance, and yet they still can be seen from here. I'm looking forward to our ride tomorrow. I wonder if Aspen is still here? I'd like to see him again. We were good riding mates.'

Clarity lay back on the soft pillows and wondered about the future and thought of some of the children at the school, and the orphanage.

'I love them and they love me too. It is a fulfilling life, yet sad too. I have no one with whom to truly share my thoughts and feelings. It is warm here in this lovely bed, yet I also recognise a loneliness. While not an ever present feeling I know it is there. And if I know this feeling now, what will it be like down the road? In two, five, and ten years? Of course Elizabeth could be right, that time will bring a man, one person with whom I can always talk, one person I can love deeply, and who will love me in the same way. This would be far more likely to happen if I had chosen a life here in England. But I did not choose the usual. Rather, my choice is a more difficult one, and it is more satisfying. Will it be emotionally fulfilling in the long term?' Clarity let herself relax completely into the large soft pillows and in moments she fell asleep.

Elizabeth awoke early to the sunlight pouring into her room. Stretching in the warmth of her bed for a moment she smiled as she thought of sharing breakfast with Clarity. Throwing back the duvet she went to the window and thrust up the sash. Elizabeth leaned out the huge window into the outdoors drinking in the early morning air. She listened to the chirping of the birds and looked up into the trees to learn which bird sang its happy song. A robin sat on the oak branch singing away to the day. 'The sky is a perfect blue', she said aloud. 'It will be a perfect day for riding.' As she went to dress her thoughts of last evening, of Clarity and of Clarity's happiness, returned. Elizabeth had not fallen immediately asleep. Rather, she had been thinking of her friend. Thoughts of Paulus ran in and out of her reflections. Paulus had been alone, lonely perhaps for a very long time. Perhaps he had only properly discovered this at lunch yesterday. How does one change or move one's life? Clarity was lonely, in a very different way. Intuitively Elizabeth placed a Beethoven CD in her Bose and let Beethoven's divine genius inspire her own musings. She returned to the open window and leaning out again into the morning, into the trees and the sunlight, breathed.

It takes a reckoning with oneself to move one's life. Thoughts were coming to her clearly now. Paulus had come to a reckoning yesterday. He was probably still digesting his discovery. Clarity was doing some of this kind of thinking too. Perhaps with Clarity it was more an expression, her reflections were most likely a natural bubbling to the surface at the right time when ready to meet the light of day. Clarity would not suppress anything. She had now gained the realisation of her feelings that it was hard living away from home, from England, from friends and a life familiar. More than this, home is comforting to one's soul. Elizabeth spoke aloud to God and his day, 'Please help me father to comfort and help my friend. If there is something I can say to her to lighten her road ahead please give me the words.'

Elizabeth and Clarity ate a light breakfast of toast, soft boiled eggs, cereal, and fruit in the sunroom.

'Aspen awaits you', Elizabeth smiled at her friend, noticing that she looked well rested.

'Oh thank you', Clarity responded. 'I was hoping to see him again and that we might be horse and rider together.'

'Good', her friend replied.

The weather was perfect for their riding day. It was 70°F and clear blue skies in the morning with a whisper of a breeze. The afternoon was warm with some summer white fluffy clouds appearing to spark Clarity's imagination. Clarity had several times pointed out the giants, the enormous faces, and the women with huge floppy hats in the clouds when they were walking their horses. Elizabeth brought up the subject of Clarity's hope of finding the emotional support, companionship, and love in a man who could share her life. Clarity quietly responded that time at Tudor Court made a world of difference.

After a good canter Elizabeth began, 'You are happy here.' Elizabeth had noticed over the course of two days together her friend relaxing into a familiar way of life.

'Yes', Clarity said slowly sighing as in grateful relief.

Elizabeth said, 'It makes me happy to know you are comfortable here.'

Clarity said, 'You and Tudor Court feel like home to me.'

Elizabeth heard a catch in Clarity's voice. She drew Chapparal up to be directly beside Aspen. As Clarity turned to look directly into Elizabeth's eyes Elizabeth saw tears welling up. Elizabeth responded with a warm loving smile and reached over to squeeze her friend's hand. After a few minutes of silently walking their horses along the bridal path by the forest Clarity spoke.

'This time at Tudor Court is making a world of difference.'

Elizabeth waited, feeling that her friend had more to say.

However when it did not come she said, 'Tomorrow we will sit in the library by the fire and read all day. We can take breaks to discuss our books. Mary will make something delicious for us and Chalmers will bring it to us. We won't budge. What do you think?'

'That sounds just right', Clarity replied softly.

That night they went to bed early. After a day outdoors with the horses they both slept soundly. The following day, Clarity's last before returning to London for her flight to Africa, they spent together in the library.

'I see why this is your favourite room', Clarity said. She had looked up from *Children of the Sahara* and seeing Elizabeth gazing out the window decided to take a break and speak.

'It has always been my favourite room, anywhere', Elizabeth replied.

Clarity continued, 'The light is just right, with the room arranged around the windows. And the books have the same effect as a lot of snow outdoors, quieting everything.'

Elizabeth responding said, 'You are right. The books absorb sound as snow does.'

Clarity continued, 'The quiet here inspires thought. Just like snow absorbs sounds and encourages the contemplation quiet offers. And the cold is an encouragement to preserve energy and encourages inward reflection.'

'Hmm, I think you have something', Elizabeth responded. 'Cold', Elizabeth repeated the word her friend had used. 'It is never cold in Africa, is it?', she asked.

'Not where I am. Though it can get very cold at night in the desert. But it is cold, in a way', Clarity said pensively. 'When you're not at home . . . as you are here . . . at home . . . as I feel here at Tudor Court . . . it can be cold. One can feel very alone.' They were silent for minutes, taking this in.

Clarity resumed. 'With the children, moments with the children can be lovely, warm, fulfilling, when they are laughing or intent on sharing something with you. They are so very present in the moment and one can not help but be very present with them.'

'Yes, I can imagine', Elizabeth responded directly and with intent to encourage her friend to continue.

'However, after the lessons are done, after the day is through and one returns to one's room, one can feel cold, sometimes I feel very cold.'

'All beauty can be absent in the cold, in the dark', Elizabeth spoke in natural and immediate response to her friend.

'Yes', Clarity nodding, confirmed her friend's understanding.

Clarity had one more night at Tudor Court. It was a warm beautiful evening. She could see the stars from her bedroom window and she felt the welcome warmth and comfort of the big canopy bed, luxurious duvet, and insuperable Egyptian cotton sheets. It was not the luxury of Tudor Court that provided the warmth and comfort she felt. She knew it to be Elizabeth and

Elizabeth's home. Tudor Court was simply a perfect reflection of Elizabeth, of Elizabeth's care and love. Elizabeth loved her home and cared for it and filled Tudor Court with her very personal warmth. Most of all Elizabeth cared for those who came to her home. Clarity felt this care. It was a care particular to her friend, a fine expression of love.

'Come back very soon', Elizabeth enthused as she hugged and held Clarity before her driver took Clarity to Heathrow.

'If for some reason I am not here when you return your room will be. It is now permanently reserved for you my dear. I have told all the staff.' Elizabeth gave her friend a warm smile and a loving kiss.

'Thank you Elizabeth. God bless you', responded Clarity.

'God bless you dear Clarity.'

CHAPTER TEN

THE CASE OF PRIDE UNDONE

CONTINUED

Elizabeth sat at her writing desk in the library. Her invitations were neatly placed to one side, and in front of her were two sets of paper and envelope yet to be addressed. The sun came in and out from hiding as large white fluffy clouds passed overhead. She had been sitting at her desk for some time and could not see the sun from her position though the sudden changes in the light in the room announced clouds. The sky from where she sat was blue and the clouds in the distance were white, no threat of rain today.

Morris entered the room. Surprised to see Elizabeth, he said, 'Oh, excuse me Mamam, I didn't realise you were still here.'

'I'm here longer than I expected to be', Elizabeth smiled at her housekeeper.

'I can check the room later', Morris said and went out, closing the door.

Elizabeth got up from her comfortable chair and went to the large south facing window and stood looking out and thinking.

'What am I contemplating? It's something I've not done before. I invite guests, they come, they mingle, converse, and it goes as it does. This was not the case in full for Elizabeth so naturally and completely thought of her guests that she was no longer conscious of the care she took in the combination of invitations she sent for any given gathering. 'Now I want to arrange, well, not quite arrange, . . . rather guide two of my guests together. Why? Why, after all these gatherings, am I seriously considering doing this? In fact it is past the point of considering, I am planning to do this.'

Elizabeth watched as the clouds moving across the sky played with the light. She thought of the two people she had in mind and she knew why she was doing this. There had been a change in Paulus. When he had left the table at luncheon last month she had thought he would not join them again. Yet, he had rejoined them. He'd come out to the garden and sat down right beside Clarity. Clarity is someone with whom Paulus would have had nothing in common. Yet he had looked comfortable there beside her. His conversation with Patricia Weatherby, and about gardening, that wasn't like Paulus either. His look of appreciation for Patricia's words of guidance and encouragement about gardening struck me. Then his call thanking me and not just for the invitation. He'd made astute comments about Clarity's sense of life, and Mrs Weatherby's kindness, yes . . . Paulus had been reflecting, and his reflection has led him to . . . a new place. It was as Paulus had dropped a heavy mantel he'd been wearing a long time, all his life I imagine and he must be about seventy.

A few minutes passed and the other person came back into her mind, Suzanne Abbington-French. Suzanne was almost twenty years younger than Paulus. She has been single all her life too. Suzanne is unaffected, humble really, quite herself, comfortable in being her own person. I have a feeling she could quite appreciate Paulus. And he would benefit very much. Suddenly the sunlight came through the window in full strong beams. Elizabeth looked up, not a cloud in the sky. She smiled. And the warmth of the sunbeams made her completely comfortable with her little plan. If things went well at the dinner she knew a larger affair, a small ball, would be in order. She went directly to her desk, wrote out her last two invitations, addressed the envelopes, placed them with the others, collected them up, and left the library.

'Is Clarity Freeman able to attend Mamam?', asked Morris as he and his mistress stood together surveying the table for dinner.

'No, she is in Africa', Elizabeth replied with a note of regret in her voice. Elizabeth had invited Clarity to the dinner party in case for some reason she might be back from Africa. 'However Bartholomew Atwater has said he will come. He is such a good sport. That will keep the numbers even but with one extra man. That will be alright, don't you think?'

'Oh yes Miss Elizabeth. Mr Atwater is a lovely man, the best of company', Morris heartily replied.

Elizabeth laughed, 'Yes he is. He will add a great old fashioned warmth to the evening.' Then she said under her breath, 'And that will help a couple of people relax', and, unspoken, get to know one another.

'Are you satisfied with the table Mamam?', Morris asked after they had completed the full circuit of the twelve settings.

'Yes Morris', and then Elizabeth hesitated. She asked, 'Do you think it generally best to seat two people beside one another or across from one another if', Elizabeth, hesitating again said, 'if you want them to get to know each other better?'

'Oh beside one another', Morris did not hesitate. 'Particularly if it is a man and a woman', he was definite.

'Why is that?', Elizabeth asked.

'Because Mamam, a man and a woman sitting beside each other will get a feel for one another. It's not as easily done across the table.'

Elizabeth laughed, 'Of course. You are right Morris. Thank you.' And she smiled at her housekeeper in appreciation.

Morris's eyes twinkled with delight in being able to be of service to his mistress, and he realised then, too, to Mr Pedigree.

That evening Elizabeth's guests duly arrived. Paulus Pedigree was in fine form, looking younger, dapper, in a new suit and tie.

'You're in fine form Paulus', Elizabeth said greeting him warmly.

As he took her hand he beamed a vital energy she had not seen in him before.

'Thank you for including me. Isn't it a fine evening. Did you see the full moon?', he enthused.

Just then Suzanne Abbington-French was ushered in to the entrance foyer. Chalmers announced, 'Miss Abbington-French.'

'Suzanne, I'm happy to see you', Elizabeth warmly greeted her guest as she moved forward to meet her and taking her arm whisked her over to where Paulus was standing.

'Paulus tells me the moon is full and clear this evening. Have you seen it?', she asked of Suzanne as the three stood together.

'Yes, it is lovely', Suzanne replied with feeling. 'She is standing right over Tudor Court.'

'Come let's see', Elizabeth responded and taking their arms in hers led the way to the large drawing room where they could gain the outdoors through the walk out windows. Moving to open one window, Elizabeth left the two standing together and smiled to herself as Morris's words came back to her. Elizabeth walked directly out onto the terrace and went to the stone balustrade to look up to the moon. Paulus and Suzanne came out together and joined her.

'There is a yellow tinge to her tonight', Suzanne said.

'Yes. And the craters are so clear. Can you see the dark patch on the left', Paulus asking Suzanne, and leaning a little closer to her, pointed.

'Do you mean the longish dark patch?', she asked.

'Yes. That is Aristotles', Paulus replied.

Elizabeth smiled and then said, 'I think I heard the bell, do excuse me.'

Her guests nodded, and continued in their conversation.

Elizabeth floated down the hall toward the entry, happy with a sense that the evening was already off to a propious beginning.

Elizabeth had arranged the seating. She sat at head of table with Bartholomew at her right and Sir Joshua Tilling on her left. Paulus Pedigree sat beside Bartholomew with Suzanne on his right. Syril Arlington sat on her right. Suzanne knew Syril and he would be a comfortable alternate dinner partner if she and Paulus did not make friends. Lady Jane Samuel sat on Arlington's right. And on Lady Jane's other side, and as other head of table, was Jack Blenheim. She and Blenheim travelled in similar circles and there would be plenty of conversation between them. Across from Lady Jane was Hale Fenwick, he too was within her circle. On Fenwick's right sat Alison Martin, beside her Elliot Newman, these two had met on their last occasion at Tudor Court. Esther White sat on Newman's right, across from Paulus and on Sir Joshua's left. Elizabeth had decided these were the arrangements likely to make for the most comfortable and satisfying evening.

'A toast', Jack Blenheim raised his crystal wine goblet and looking down the table with a smile for his dinner companions said, 'To Elizabeth, the most gracious hostess or host in England outside Buckingham Palace', he finished heartily.

'To Elizabeth', the guests responded. All but Elizabeth drank their toast.

After her guests had drunk their toast, some of whom took another appreciative swallow, Elizabeth said, 'Thank you. May I join you now in drinking this splendid wine?' And she suited the action to the word. Smiling at Hale Fenwick, she raised her glass, 'To Hale who has brought us this fine wine. I know you have an excellent cave, and this is most excellent indeed. To Hale's good taste, and generosity.'

All raised their glasses again, 'To Hale', happily imbibing the wine.

'This is excellent wine. Burgundy '25 perhaps', said Sir Joshua.

'It's the best I've had', responded Bartholomew, taking another drink. 'My goodness I've almost finished my glass', he said disappointedly.

Elizabeth gave an almost imperceptible nod to the wine steward who was standing to the side. In a moment he arrived at table pouring more wine for Barthlomew. Eyeing the rest of the company he moved across to Elliot Newman who obviously had been enjoying the wine just as much and refilled his glass.

'Oh thank you my dear chap. One must enjoy such fine libations', Barthlomew said after helping himself to a good swallow.

Elizabeth and Sir Joshua laughed simultaneously at Atwater's enjoyment. Then all three laughed together.

Another servant brought the soup and began ladling the vegetable purée into the guests' Spode soup bowls. Elizabeth looked down the table to Suzanne and Paulus. They appeared to be enjoying themselves in a conversation with Elliot Newman, Alison Martin, and Syril Arlington. Alison Martin, usually calm and reserved, was quite animated. Suddenly she and Suzanne were laughing. Syril was smiling broadly. Newman, when pausing from imbibing his wine, was adding to their laughter with what he was saying. Paulus, while somewhat quiet, was also a part of the group. He was listening attentively and Elizabeth also noted looking admiringly at Suzanne.

Bartholomew winked at Elizabeth. She took up her wine glass to stifle a verbal response, which she then spoke to herself, 'Oh you know then.' She glanced at Sir Joshua to see if he knew too that she had set Suzanne and Paulus up together, but Sir Joshua was enjoying his soup. Elizabeth looked back at Bartholomew who was now discreetly eating. But he gave her a sideways glance as he dipped his spoon, and his look was as to say, 'Come now, we are old friends, I know how you think.'

The main course of local pheasant, fresh herbs and vegetables from Elizabeth's garden and prepared by her most able cook was much enjoyed by all. Fenwick's wine continued to flow. Elizabeth and Bartholomew enjoyed Sir Joshua's tales on diplomacy in foreign countries and, a time or two spent at Windsor and Balmoral. One of the tales included Prince Henry and the Lord Mayor's daughter. Apparently after a date the Prince had invited her back to Buckingham Palace. When she went to leave the Palace gates were locked and she had to stay the night. In the morning when the maid arrived to open the draperies and deliver morning tea she hid under the duvet.

After Bartholomew's comment Elizabeth had refrained from looking over to Suzanne and Paulus too frequently. However she had noticed that the conversation on their side of the table had quieted and the two of them had been tete-a-tete since the main course. At about the same time Elliot Newman had been most gentlemanly and had turned to Esther White to engage her. Esther, a quiet and most capable financier, would have been quite content to enjoy her meal. However Elliot, being the fine gentleman he was reputed to be, easily included her in conversation. As Elizabeth had anticipated Hale Fenwick and Jack Blenheim engaged Lady Jane and the other end of the table was well occupied.

After the dinner plates had been removed and before dessert arrived Lady Jane said to the whole company, 'Jack, Hale, and I have enjoyed your excellent meal and this lovely company so well that we have decided we must reciprocate and invite you all to another dinner in my home. We hope you will accept.'

Elliot Newman and Sir Joshua raised their glasses simultaneously, 'Here here.' And then all at table did likewise. Elizabeth raised her glass in particular to Lady Jane, thanking her with her eyes and a smile for her graciousness.

The guests rose from table about an hour after the completion of the meal and all moved to the drawing room to continue conversations. Elizabeth was very pleased to see Paulus and Suzanne sit down together on the small chesterfield, well engaged in conversation.

Lady Jane sat herself next to Elizabeth. 'I am enjoying your evening very much Elizabeth', she said. 'Hale and I know each other's families but have not had the chance to get to know each other. This was a lovely opportunity to begin to change that.'

'I'm so pleased to hear that', Elizabeth replied.

Lady Jane continued, 'We would like to arrange that dinner. However I do not want it to conflict with any of your plans.'

'Are you thinking of a time?', Elizabeth asked.

'Yes. We were thinking six weeks or so before Christmas.'

'That sounds very good, there is no conflict', Elizabeth smiled. 'Perhaps I will have a New Year ball and invite the same people we are enjoying so well', Elizabeth said.

Lady Jane smiled, 'That sounds perfectly lovely.'

Paulus and Suzanne were the last guests to leave. They had sat together all evening, not stirring from their contented place on the chesterfield for two in the drawing room. When it was time to leave Paulus took Suzanne out to her car.

'I hope we may see one another again soon. This has been a most enjoyable evening', Paulus said. And then added slowly, 'In particular because of your company.'

Suzanne was looking directly at him, responding to his gaze with her open face and a warm smile. Then responding to his words said, 'Yes. I've enjoyed myself too, very much.' She paused. Paulus waited.

'Would you like to come to my house, perhaps tomorrow? If you'd like I can give you a tour of the house and grounds. It is nothing like Tudor Court, but it is my home and I love it', Suzanne said simply.

'I'd like that very much', Paulus said, happily.

'Shall we say 2PM then?', Suzanne suggested.

'I'll see you then', Paulus replied and waited for her to seat herself in her car, bowed his head slightly to her, and closed her car door.

Paulus drove slowly home replaying the evening and contemplating his time with Suzanne. He was smiling contentedly, happy. He parked his car and instead of going straight into the house Paulus stood on the gravel drive looking at his house and its setting. He was doing this more often recently, this time in the moonlight. 'I'd like this to be a home, not merely a house', he said aloud to the house, the trees, and to the place where he stood. He sent his request up to God.

The following day Paulus rose early. Instead of lingering in the warmth of his bed as soon as he awoke he got out of bed to begin his day. The thought of seeing Suzanne moved his spirit to a new and higher level. As he shaved he studied his face in the mirror.

'Yes I am seventy. However I think I can give myself some credit for looking' . . . trying to be realistic he gave his face a reassessment . . . 'can I say sixty four? Yes I can', he smiled. 'And I am pretty fit.' This was true. Paulus did a lot of work on his property, certainly the few acres directly around the house. He mowed grass, did carpentry jobs, the old barn had recently needed some new boards, and he'd done some planting with Rufus. Paulus had not acquired the habit of eating more than he needed. Perhaps more important to his appearance was that he was happier. In the last little while, and he knew it stemmed from that time with Elizabeth and Clarity, something had knocked on his door and he had answered. Pride was on the way out making room for a nimbleness to enter. Pride was in his way, pride had been a barrier to relationship and importantly to his relationship with himself. In some way, not entirely, not yet, he had overcome the barrier and was on a new path. And Suzanne was on this path. I am looking forward to Suzanne's tour of her home. I wonder, is it a home? Or a house? That will be interesting to learn. She has been single too, at least not married I know, all her life. Can one make a home on one's own?

As Paulus pleasantly anticipated his afternoon with Suzanne, Suzanne was taking extra care at Meadowfield. Meadowfield, as with Elizabeth and Tudor Court, had been left to her. When in her twenties her grandfather had left the house and property to her, there had been much discussion by her mother and father as to whether she should sell it. Suzanne, surprised by her grandfather's gift, had been just as delighted as her parents were concerned by the thought of their daughter living in the countryside. Her mother was much against Suzanne living on her own and in the country.

'My dear', Suzanne well remembered her mother's words, 'If you move into your own home in your twenties, what will a man have to offer you? Meadowfield is a lovely house with beautiful grounds and out in the country. You won't want to leave. And where will you meet people?' But Suzanne's reply was, 'Mum, perhaps your father knew me better. Meadowfield suits me well. I believe grandfather thought about what he was doing, and I know I can be happy there.' And she had been very happy for more than twenty five years.

Suzanne had been moving from room to room checking for she knew not what. She was an organised person and all was as she knew it would be, in order. She stopped in her favourite room, the smaller drawing room, where one wall facing the gardens was three quarters window. She said to herself, I am looking at everything, at each room, to try and see how Paulus will see it. She laughed at herself. And with her hands on the back of her favourite chesterfield, the thick cotton fabric of a garden floral pattern she'd chosen from a wonderful old furniture shoppe in London, her first furniture purchase, she smiled, satisfied. From this chesterfield one had a fine view of green trees, green grasses, deep burgundy snap dragons, bedding plants, birds, squirrels, and the sky. I wonder if Paulus will notice. She hoped he would.

Paulus arrived at two o'clock. He smiled as he drove in the front gate. 'I timed it perfectly', he spoke aloud. 'It is funny driving in the front gate when I've driven by many times in the past and noticed the Meadowfield square beige plaque overhead with its lettering in appropriately faded gold.'

The house was visible from the entrance gate and as he drove in to park he wondered how old it was. He guessed it was about one hundred and seventy five years. It was of moderate size, perhaps large for one person. But he had a feeling that it was just right for Suzanne. He got out of his Land Rover and took his time looking about. He wanted to learn all he could of Suzanne and he had a feeling that Meadowfield was very much her own.

The pebbles of the drive, for it was not the more common gravel sort, had a tinge of colour, a tinge of green. The drive was not large. Most of the area fronting the house had been given over to the trees, bushes, and flowerbeds. She loves colour, he said to himself and particularly green. He walked slowly toward the house, studying it. The windows were large and trimmed all in white, a well painted and well kept white. Some vines had been allowed to grow a small distance up from the ground but were kept below the windows. The overall look of the house, painted a pale yellow planted amongst trees and green, was one of warmth and welcome. It was a happy place Paulus thought, smiling. Paulus stepped up the stairs to the large oak door. The door opened.

'Hello. I was watching for you', Suzanne said openly smiling. Paulus felt her warm, open welcome.

'Thank you', he beamed and as Suzanne stepped back he stepped inside.

He stood in a roomy foyer and a large window on the other end of the house drew his eye immediately. He could see through to the trees, and he supposed, garden. The setting of the window made the outdoors present. As he stood, while Suzanne took his jacket, he took in the whole feel of the house.

'This is a home', he said aloud.

Suzanne turned back to him from where she had been about to hang his jacket in an armoire.

She smiled warmly, and patting his jacket flat against herself said, 'Please, come in.'

Suzanne showed Paulus every room. She hadn't planned it so but Paulus's interest led her on and they both enjoyed the tour. When she brought him to the small drawing room she said nothing. She wanted very much to learn his response to her favourite room.

'You spend more time here', he said as if it were knowledge to him.

'How do you know?', she asked surprised and delighted.

He moved toward the large window looking out to the garden bordered by enormous old beech trees. He placed his hands on the back of the chesterfield and stood there taking in the beauty of the scene from the window. Suzanne stepped forward and stood beside him. They stood for many moments both looking out upon a sea of green and the beautiful garden of colourful flowers. Paulus turned to her and looking into her eyes leaned over and kissed her. He looked again into her eyes and then back out to the green's of the earth and to the blue of the sky. They stood together silently appreciating the beauty of the moment.

That night, for Paulus and Suzanne only said goodbye that evening, Paulus came to a decision. I'm going to ask her to marry me he said firmly to himself. This direct simple statement stopped him with the thought, I have never asked a woman to marry me. And he sat down on the nearest chair. He envisioned the time they had had together, standing close together in her favourite room, going out to her garden, walking and talking in the garden, going back to the house, sitting in her favourite room, talking. It was the feeling he had while together with

Suzanne that had made his mind up for him. It was a feeling of great comfort, a warm feeling of happiness. Many minutes passed as he sat in the brown velvet seated wood chair that backed against the hallway wall. I've never sat here, and I've not seen my home from this vantage point. 'Home?', he asked himself aloud. He suddenly realised it felt like home. How can this be? He recalled not two months ago after the afternoon luncheon at Tudor Court where in Clarity's presence he had begun to question his pride. And, when arriving back here he had stood in his driveway and first asked about home, and then again for the third time yesterday. His request had been granted. He knew it had something to do with his decision to be with Suzanne. He knew it had started with wanting to and then making an effort to reach out to Suzanne. And then, to Suzanne responding. I'd had to ask he said in realisation.

The next morning Paulus took a tour of his home, beginning again by seating himself in the velvet chair that was new to him. He sat for several minutes. Then he stood and he walked down the hall and as he did he experienced a dawning, as seeing from the other side of Niagara Falls, from the other side of the rainbow. The walls around him made him feel warmer, cozier. Cozy? This was not a word Paulus had used in the past. The furniture felt welcoming, he thought he could sit now for long stretches, stretch his legs out on an ottoman and read. He'd have to get one. The windows seemed more interesting, inviting him to step up and look out to use the sky and the vista to imagine. Imagine? Imagine what? The possibilities. The possibilities for life seemed vast now. Something had opened up inside him. Deep inside it felt different. He felt different. He felt renewed, alive. The phone rang.

'Hello', Suzanne's voice greeted him. Paulus smiled, happy.

'Hello', he said warmly.

'I just wanted to call you', she sounded like a child.

'I'm happy you did', he responded.

There was a comfortable pause. Neither felt the need to talk.

Then Paulus spoke, 'I'd like to see you.' Then he said, 'I have something to ask you.'

'You can come any time', she replied.

'May I come today?', he asked.

'Yes', she said.

'I'll come at three', Paulus returned.

'Good. I'll see you then', and in another moment she had rung off.

He put down the receiver. Almost not recognising himself, yet knowing this was right, and that he, the renewed Paulus, was now leading the way. He didn't think about it, nor Suzanne, for the rest of the morning. After something to eat, he put on his Wellington's and went out the back door to be outside.

He dead headed some petunia's that he noticed needed attention. His trees all looked healthy, he also noticed. The sky was blue with clouds, white, not grey. While it was damp underfoot it was unlikely to rain. This was the day he would propose marriage. He flung his head back and looked up to the sky. He opened his arms wide, if not to the world, to life. And Paulus cried out, 'Life is grand. All the possibilities. I'm not going to miss them anymore.'

He started running. He ran down the path leading away from the house to the open field beyond. He ran into the field, almost tripping. He laughed aloud. In a few moments he stopped, stood, and turned slowly three hundred and sixty degrees to take in the life around him, nature in all her beauty, and life in all its glory. Life is grand. It is wonderful. He felt alive. 'It is good to be alive', Paulus announced.

'Shall we tell Elizabeth first?', Suzanne asked Paulus.

Suzanne had responded to Paulus's proposal immediately, with 'Yes.' Then she had placed her head on his shoulder. It was such a nice fit, too, they both felt it.

'Do you want to ring her up?', asked Paulus.

'No, we should go to Tudor Court to see her and tell her in person', said Suzanne.

'When?', he replied.

'Oh, let's go now', Suzanne said like a child wanting to knock on a friend's door to have her come out to play.

Paulus smiled, 'Yes.'

The two drove to Tudor Court and arrived late afternoon. Suzanne skipped up the stone steps to the broad oak door. She turned beaming at Paulus, waiting for him to join her before sounding the brass knocker. Paulus felt pride, the right kind of pride, for this wonderful woman who had agreed to marry him. He arrived by her side. She sounded the knocker.

Paulus knew, and now articulated to himself, that it was Elizabeth they had to thank for this happy time and for the happy prospect. It was not their meeting in Elizabeth's home for which they had her to thank, for they may well have met elsewhere. It was the opportunity of experiencing Elizabeth's love of life and seeing it on display in Elizabeth’s relationship with Clarity. It was this that had awoken Paulus to his pride, the pride that had been killing all his relationships, including with himself. It was this awakening to the effect of the killer pride that had brought Paulus back to life. Reflection had enabled Paulus to see himself for who he was and courage had been required to look to who he could be. Courage had allowed him to face reality, a necessity for moving to a better path for life.

The door opened and Chalmers standing on the threshold greeted them.

'Good day Miss Abbington-French, Mr Pedigree', the capable Chalmers, not expecting them, did remember them.

'Oh Chalmers do tell us that Elizabeth is at home', Suzanne bubbled over with a happy energized spirit.

'Yes Mamam, Miss Fennington is at home. Shall I tell her you wish to see her?', Chalmers asked in a kindly way having registered Suzanne's eagerness.

'Oh would you Chalmers? Please', Suzanne replied.

Most aware and astute, Chalmers almost winked at Paulus but refrained.

And stepping back to allow them both to come forward, he said, 'I will be just a moment. Please make yourselves comfortable', and he moved with purpose down the hall.

In the foyer, Paulus stood admiring the artwork. Suzanne with a restless excitement moved about. She touched a chair back, not wanting to sit, fingered a frame of an eighteenth century oil painting not noticing the subject. She took a few steps forward and a couple of steps back. Elizabeth came gliding down the hallway toward them, hands outstretched to greet them both with a warm personal welcome.

'What a lovely surprise', she said before reaching them. Then as she reached them she touched each of their arms simultaneously saying, 'Thank you for thinking of me', beaming a warm happy smile, sharing in their energy.

'We just had to come and tell you. We wanted you to be the first to know', Suzanne breathlessly bubbled forth.

'Come, come into the parlour', as Elizabeth spoke she guided them toward the parlour. Opening the door she ushered them toward the chesterfield for two, closed the door, and sat directly in front of them in a beautiful brocaded Louis XVI armchair.

When Chalmers arrived in the library, where Elizabeth had been reading Samuel Eliot Morison's *The Oxford History of the American People*, he had announced her visitors. While a visit at the moment was a surprise, she had not been surprised to learn of the two people together at her door. She waited only a moment now to hear Suzanne tell her of their engagement.

'We are engaged to be married', Suzanne said, her voice energized and alive with happiness . . . 'Paulus asked me this afternoon. We wanted you to be the first to know', she finished with a broad smile.

'How wonderful', Elizabeth responded vibrantly.

'Congratulations Paulus', Elizabeth turned to him, her felicitation all the warmer for her offering of the formal and classic traditional response to learning of an engagement. She turned to Suzanne and taking her hands in her own said, 'I am very happy for you Suzanne. And in adding to Paulus's happiness', she looked to him for a moment and then back to Suzanne, 'you will add to your own in a way I believe that will make your own complete.'

'Thank you Elizabeth', Suzanne said softly.

This was a happy moment, the three sitting together in appreciation.

Then Paulus spoke, 'We have you to thank Elizabeth. This would not have been possible,' and he took Suzanne's hand, 'but for your including me in your and Clarity's company. I learned through you that a heart to be true is open and that honesty is its natural friend. Pride blocks this openness and remains an entrenched barrier to true relationship. I did not know myself. My pride had come between myself and the image of myself pride had cultivated for me. It was a hard realisation and very hard to think about. I had spent my life valuing the wrong things, looking in the wrong direction, living the wrong life. Thankfully reckoning with reality led to clarity to see my pride and let it go.' He looked at Suzanne and squeezed her hand.

Suzanne was very happy. She had someone who needed her, and whose love would grow with time. Paulus had a new lease on life.

Elizabeth, with a full smile said, 'I am very happy. Thank you for your kind and generous words. I feel privileged that you have come personally like this to tell me and that I may share in your happiness.'

They rose. They stood together another few moments basking in the warmth the three of them shared together. Elizabeth walked them to the main door. Saying goodbye and exchanging promises to see one another again soon, they parted happy and appreciative of all good things.

CHAPTER ELEVEN

THE MONTH OF DECEMBER

Lady Jane Samuel's dinner in early November had been a distinctive occasion. True to her word she had invited all those who attended Elizabeth's dinner in September. Many other guests were included and for all the noble names the dinner was a relaxed and most enjoyable affair. Importantly, from Elizabeth's perspective, Paulus and Suzanne had had a lovely opportunity to be together in the company of friends and good people. It had pleased Elizabeth very much to see them again, happy, relaxed, comfortable, enjoying and appreciating life.

Directly following Elizabeth's dinner party where Lady Jane had decided on the November dinner Elizabeth decided on a ball for New Year. Elizabeth started preparing her invitation list early. As soon as her list was complete she began addressing invitations, which took three and a half weeks. All the invitations were mailed by late October and then Elizabeth turned her attention to arranging for the orchestra. She knew she wanted The Tony Mildorell Orchestra. She laughed when she thought of Tony. The smooth voiced Italian singer had put together a fabulous orchestra, Brit's and Americans who played to perfection the Glenn Miller, Tommy Dorsey, and Duke Ellington hits with

Tony fancing himself as another Tony Bennett. If his orchestra could come the ball would be a success.

'Hello Tony. It's Elizabeth Fennington.'

There was only a slight pause on the end of the line, 'Elizabeth, your happy voice, full of life, makes me happy too', he enthused in his northern Italian accent. 'It is good to hear you again. How are you and how is that beautiful Tudor Court of yours?', he asked with his Italian charm and vivacity.

'We are both very well, thank you. And I'm hoping you and your superb orchestra would enjoy another visit to Tudor Court', Elizabeth said with her own charming warmth.

'Ohh?', Tony said slowly, and she could hear his smile.

'Yes, I am holding a ball at New Year', she said.

'Are you?', Tony replied, still slowly, with a little quizzical lilt in his voice.

'Yes . . .', Elizabeth, about to explain more precisely that she wanted to hire Tony and his orchestra for the evening, stopped. She realised that Tony, usually very quick to pick up his cues, was playing with her.

'Tony . . . what is it?'

He began to laugh, 'Miss Elizabeth, I know of your ball. And I was thinking you would ask me, or should I say', Tony was trying to be humble, 'I was hoping you would ask us to play for you.'

Elizabeth laughed, 'How did you know?'

'Hale Fenwick. He called on behalf of his cousin who hosts the Fenwick reunion and we are booked for his occasion. He asked if we were playing for your ball. So I waited, hoping you'd call,' he was humble now with openness about his preference for Elizabeth and Tudor Court. 'Tudor Court is beautiful. And we love the countryside there and the day after we always have a good time outdoors whatever the weather. We love to play for you and your guests.'

'Thank you Tony. Did you really wait?'

'Oh yes. I refused three offers for New Year.'

'Well thank you very much. I will have to call you earlier next time. So you'll come?', Elizabeth smiled into the phone.

'Yes, with bells on, as they say.'

'Good. You will contact Morris again as before to have him arrange things as you like them? You still have his number?', Elizabeth asked.

'Yes Mamam', Tony had gone into his business mode.

When they completed their arrangements and Elizabeth had rung off she sat back at her desk for a moment and felt herself beginning to relax again. Arrangements were made, Morris and Mary would take good care that all would be in readiness. And now she could herself look forward to the ball.

Elizabeth had the month of December to herself. However Tudor Court was not completely quiet as her staff began organising for the New Year ball. While there were no guests to welcome and consider Elizabeth was thinking about what would make for a fine time and contribute to a good start to the New Year for all who would be attending the ball.

Elizabeth spent many happy December hours in her library reading. She was reading; Bagehot's *The English Constitution*, Mark Twain's *Huckleberry Finn*, *The Autobiography of Benjamin*

Franklin, and Winston Churchill's *The River War*. Many times she'd look up to the south facing window and think of a New Year's guest and to whom he or she must be introduced, to whom she must say a word about this or that. Each time she thought of Paulus and Suzanne Elizabeth smiled and easily imagining their happiness took pleasure in imagining all to which they had to look forward.

Normally when Elizabeth was in the library her staff did not disturb her. However a knock on the door sounded many times in December. Mary Lemes, Elizabeth's cook, rarely came to the library. However in her preparations for New Year she came twice. Would the mistress like a main meat dish on the buffet? And the second time, would Mamam want an additional dessert, a special large cake Mary had in mind as celebration after midnight. To the former Mary received a no, to the latter a yes. Mary was satisfied. Morris came too to the library. Given two hundred and fifty guests, more chairs should be made available. He suggested chairs be arranged along the walls in the hall outside the Great Room. This way guests resting from dancing or wanting a chat could be accommodated. Elizabeth agreed. Would Morris have enough chairs? Morris, having anticipated Elizabeth's agreement, had canvassed the house. Thirty six chairs that could be used could be brought from other parts of the house and from storage to the hallway outside the Great Room and to the large drawing room down from the Great Room. Morris anticipated a need for perhaps eighty chairs, for about a third of the guests at any one time. But guests could also rest or chat in the nearby rooms. Another twenty chairs along the hall would suffice Morris thought. Mr Blumun, their immediate neighbour, had offered the additional twenty chairs.

'How did Emmett learn of your need?', Elizabeth asked Morris, always curious to learn of the ingenuity of her staff.

'Our Tom Mamam was talking with his Ernie and as Mr Blumun is always invited to your large parties Tom let slip the plans', Morris said with a smile he could not help.

'Very good Morris', Elizabeth laughed.

'Yes Mamam,' her most organised housekeeper replied. Morris had anticipated his questions and had only to knock once.

Ellen, whose job it is to keep her mistress's wardrobe in order had asked about her dress for New Year.

'Will you be wearing black Mamam?', Ellen asked.

'What do you think Ellen? There will be a lot of black that evening. My guests should be able to distinguish me should they have a need to speak with me', Elizabeth wanted Ellen's input.

'Oh I don't think there will be any problem there. Mamam is naturally distinguished', Ellen took good pride in her mistress's appearance.

Elizabeth smiled, 'Thank you Ellen. I'm thinking of something brighter something with colour.'

Ellen paused, thinking, scanning in her mind's eye her mistress's wardrobe. Then she said, 'There is the burgundy full length Givenchy Mamam.'

'Yes', Elizabeth pondered. 'I wonder if a I need to go shopping', she frowned. Elizabeth was not a shopper.

'Then, there is the soft mauve silk and cotton Diana Von Furstenberg', Ellen was trying to help her mistress avoid shopping if possible.

'That's the one', Elizabeth responded immediately, assuredly. 'Thank you Ellen. The mauve is the one, and no shopping', she smiled.

Ellen smiled back, happy to have thought of the right dress, and to have saved her mistress the irritating task of having to go to the shoppes and of searching, particularly in this season.

Elizabeth moved from her desk to her favourite chair, a large low comfortable chair that faced the south window. Her father had had two of these chairs especially made, he called them old lawyers' chairs. When she'd asked about them he had told her how he'd discovered the chair in an old lawyers' club in New York. The club library had a number of these great leather backed and seated wood framed chairs that had been designed for sitting at long stretches reading dull dry texts. As a necessity against dozing the chairs were lower to the ground by a third of a regular dimensioned chair. One could comfortably stretch one's legs out full length without a bend in the knee. These two chairs her father had always used when reading. She sat gazing out the broad open paned window with the *Claremont Review of Books* in her lap, her legs out full stretch. The sun would be going down soon and she'd have to move to the west window to see it. But for the moment she could watch the light change from her favourite chair.

Elizabeth imagined the ball. The music would be wonderful, all her favourite old music, dance music, the music her father had loved. My first dance was in Tudor Court's Great Room with Daddy. I must have been eleven or twelve. Daddy asked me to dance and then waited for me to accept. Surprised, I had nodded. He took my hand and led me to the centre of the floor. At first we went slowly. I remember him saying just listen and move to the music. And so I did. He led, and I followed, listening to the music, I loved it. Then we went faster, Elizabeth laughed as a thought came to her. I think the band leader was keeping an eye on Daddy and me. Because once I'd caught on to the particular beat, a new one sounded in my ears and we'd move to that. It was wonderful swirling, twirling with Daddy. She laughed again. Daddy could dance.

Elizabeth came back to the present. Paulus and Suzanne will dance all evening together in the Great Room. It will be good to see them happy and enjoying themselves. With whom will I dance? The question surprised her. All the men who dance will ask me. Hale Fenwick and Jack Blenheim will ask. My neighbour Emmett Blumun, who I know does not like dancing, will ask his hostess for one dance. And it will be Blumun's only dance for the evening.

Yet now she recognised something else was there in that question, with whom will I dance? The question clarified itself in her mind. With whom do I want to dance? To this question no answer came. She rose from the low comfortable chair and went to the west window and stood. The sky was coloured with the last light of day, pale orange, light pink. The light coming through white clouds behind the setting sun made a burst of beams as though behind a throne which they were meant to light. The beams of light in the heavens lit Elizabeth's mind. Will I be single all my life? Watching the light she knew who and what it represented. She waited.

Do I wish to be single, she wondered. She thought of Paulus. He likely had not considered his state all his years . . . until that day when something dawned. The colours behind the bright white beams of sunlight playing along the clouds were deeper orange and pink now. That day, yes, the day I saw the change in his face was the day Clarity was here. He had recognised his pride. And he let it go. Pride. Do I have pride? Undue pride? I don't think it's pride. Is it a serious independence? A lack of vulnerability? A lack of vulnerability might come from pride. The beams of light disappeared as the sun sank below the horizon.

Why am I thinking about this? Suzanne and Paulus keep coming to mind. I am happy for them and, . . . I wonder at happiness shared. And thoughts of her enjoyment of Tudor Court in the first year came to her. The quiet, the peace, time to myself, time with books, writing, and the beauty of the grounds. And time to fully value all of that. Something had dawned upon me at the end of that time. It was getting dark now. It had something to do with that time I had had. Time to appreciate.

That appreciation was an appreciation for life and one's own gift of life. And it led to a desire for greater appreciation of others. My guests now, and from the beginning, have enjoyed themselves at Tudor Court. Some have learned something valuable about life through time here. And Paulus's expressing directly his appreciation of having met Clarity here, and what it meant to him, the gift of Suzanne, means something to me. That gift is his being able to receive Suzanne. If I'm thinking about this there is something there. There is something I at least have to uncover. Is it pride?

That night Elizabeth got down on her knees by her bed to pray, as she had been taught as a child. As she knelt a feeling of humbleness came to her.

'This is an unfamiliar feeling yet not unwelcome. It is a feeling I do not recall having before. Perhaps pride did not appear in me as a child. After she said her prayers which she always had done but not kneeling, not since childhood, instead of getting into bed she pottered about her room taking in the feeling, thinking.

Getting down on one's knees is physically humbling. In that physical act is recognition, recognition that there is one superior to oneself and, that control of all matters does not lie with oneself. And this sense gives one pause to consider. If I feel this humbling, a difference in my normal attitude or view, then there is something here, and pressing her hand to her breast, aloud Elizabeth said, 'I have left something unconsidered. There is something I have not learned.'

CHAPTER TWELVE

THE BALL

The evening of the ball arrived. At the last moment Clarity called, having arrived back from Africa and hearing of the Tudor Court ball asked if she could attend.

'Oh Clarity how wonderful that you are here, of course my dear. I am so happy you are home, and that you will come', Elizabeth excited to hear Clarity's voice bubbled forth with eagerness, and in anticipation of seeing her friend.

'Wonderful. Thank you Elizabeth, I so look forward to hearing you tell me in person of how you are.'

'Good. Your room will be waiting. Stay as long as you like', Elizabeth replied, smiling. Clarity, sensing Elizabeth's smile, laughing said, 'Alright I will!' The two laughed together.

Elizabeth had gone shopping. She stood before her full length mirror in a deep green gown with the hint of a shimmering trim edging the sleeveless arms and the hem of the full length dress. The sparkle accentuated the lustre of her hair and the healthy glow of her clear skin.

'What do you think Ellen?', she asked her maid.

Ellen had laid out the mauve gown they had originally discussed along with the new green gown. 'Mamam looks lovely, simply lovely. The mauve suits you well. But this is New Year Mamam, and the green is a gown to celebrate in', Ellen replied.

'Yes, yes you are right. It is New Year and we should sparkle. A new year is upon us and we must meet it, greet it, and engage with it', Elizabeth laughed, surprising herself a little with this effusive response.

Ellen smiled at her mistress and said with enthusiasm, 'Yes Mamam.'

'I was going to take the gown off and come back in an hour to dress again. But I am going to wear it now. I'll go and say hello to Tony and his orchestra', Elizabeth said happily.

Ellen nodded, 'Your shoes Mamam', and handed Elizabeth the soft green satin low pumps that matched the gown beautifully.

'Thank you', Elizabeth responded, slipping them on. 'They are light and comfortable.'

'Perfect for dancing Mamam', Ellen said kindly, smiling.

'Yes, thank you Ellen', Elizabeth replied softly.

As Elizabeth made her way to the Great Room she felt how much she was looking forward to dancing, to moving, to flying across the dance floor. She even had prepared a list of pieces to give Tony to ensure he would not miss the particular ones she wished to hear and to which she wished to dance.

Richard Rodgers Edelweiss Waltz
Strauss Vienna Blood
Begin the Beguine
Shostakovich The Second Waltz
Strauss Voices of Spring

Eugen Doga Grammofon
Franz Lehár The Merry Widow
The Viennese Waltz

There were not many men who could dance the Viennese Waltz well. But Hale Fenwick could, and she hoped he would ask her for this one.

Tony immediately saw Elizabeth upon her entering the Great Room. He was in conversation with a violinist and ceased speaking in order to greet her.

He spoke in his rich warm voice, 'Good evening', Tony was admiring Elizabeth's overall appeal in her gown in a requisitely Italian manner. However in front of the orchestra he refrained from saying anything.

'Good evening Tony. Your tuxedo suits you well', she paid him a compliment he deserved.

He broke into a broad smile in response.

'Everyone', and she smiled and gestured to the orchestra members, 'looks lovely', she said generously. A few of the twenty two musicians acknowledged her compliment with a smile and nodded their thank you.

'Tony, will you kindly play these few pieces? I am very much looking forward to dancing this evening', and Elizabeth gave him her list.

Tony perused the list. 'Certainly', he replied. 'I see your favourite is here, the Viennese Waltz. We will play it two or three times', he said enthusiastically. Elizabeth beamed at him.

As Elizabeth left the Great Room she saw Morris across the hall in the large drawing room where the buffet tables had been arranged. She moved to its doorway and stood in the entrance surveying the arrangement.

'Morris, everything looks just lovely. Is all as you would have it?', she asked her housekeeper.

'We decided at the last minute Mamam to set up an additional table especially for non-alcoholic drinks. I imagine there will be a lot of dancing and your guests will be thirsty', Morris said simply, gesturing to a table at an angle in a corner of the room.

'What a good idea', Elizabeth said appreciatively. 'You've rearranged things very well. The room has retained its warm atmosphere.'

'Thank you Mamam', Morris shone in his mistress's appreciation.

Chalmers appeared in the hall. 'Excuse me Mamam, Mr Fenwick has arrived and begs your pardon, but asks to speak with you. I put him in the parlour.'

'Oh, thank you Chalmers. You did right. I'll go now', replied Elizabeth.

Interesting, Elizabeth said to herself as she moved down the hallway toward the front of the house. I'm intrigued. I cannot think of what Hale has to say to me. If a friend had arrived whom he wanted to bring he would have telephoned. She swept into the parlour. Immediately Hale Fenwick stood to meet her. Chalmers had taken his outer clothing. He stood tall at six foot two, looking a physical triumph with his broad shoulders and trim body fittingly accentuated by his tuxedo. His full head of rich brown hair rested perfectly relaxed on his well formed head highlighting his handsome face.

'Hale. It is good to see you. I hope all is well', Elizabeth said, moving toward him.

'Elizabeth. Yes all is well. I have spontaneously come early and should apologize. However I see you are dressed and ready I hope for a grand evening of dancing', he said smiling as he took her hands in his pressing them warmly.

She laughed. 'Yes I am. I've been thinking how much I'm looking forward to dancing.'

'Well then let's not waste another minute', he responded with energy. 'I suggest I escort you to the Great Room and we practise along with the orchestra', he said with his lovely smile and not waiting for her reply, whisked her down the hall.

Tingling inside and laughing aloud Elizabeth said, 'I think you have called my number. I've been imagining whirling across the room to the Viennese Waltz, and I know you know the Viennese Waltz', she responded gaily.

'Then', he was laughing with her now, 'that is just what we shall do.'

They entered the Great Room arm in arm. The orchestra was practising, horns and violins were sounding their notes. Hale led them directly to the orchestra leader and said as a strong, kind, leader speaking with his army before drills, 'Tony would you begin practising the Viennese Waltz and we will practise our dancing.'

Tony smiled broadly and raising his brow looked to Elizabeth but replied to Hale, 'Yes sir', and immediately turned to his musicians, 'The Viennese Waltz.'

The music began and as the rising notes filled the Great Room Hale took his partner firmly by her waist and hand and they began to move. As they whirled and twirled around the floor, Elizabeth happy, Hale smiling in response to her, laughter rang out from the two as the violins and horns played. Around and around they danced the full expanse of the uninterrupted grandeur of the Tudor Court Great Room. Moving lightly across the open expanse of beautifully kept and polished wood floor Hale and Elizabeth danced as one to the music. The musicians, catching glimpses of them as they came by the band stand, responded with appreciative expressions. Elizabeth and Hale were riveted upon one another, necessary perhaps for dancing in close harmony. Though when the waltz was through they did not remove themselves from each other. Hale raised his hand in thanks to the orchestra as he guided Elizabeth out of the room. Neither spoke for a full minute as they moved together into the hall and down the hallway.

Then Hale said, 'Shall we greet your guests at the door as they arrive', and not as a question.

Elizabeth turned to him fully, still smiling, glowing, from the exhilaration of the dance. She looked into his eyes and without speaking to his unasked question responded affirmatively. And so they stood side by side greeting each guest, couple, or group of guests as they arrived. If people were surprised to see Hale standing by Elizabeth they did not indicate either in word or facial expression.

And so the evening went, Elizabeth and Hale side by side. They moved as one from the dance floor to the buffet. They sat together eating or enjoying a drink. She sat and he went to the buffet or the bar bringing two plates and two sets of silverware or two glasses of Champagne. It was in these moments when Elizabeth was alone that her guests came up to her to speak, to comment on the orchestra, the dancing, the evening, or to speak to something they'd been wanting to tell her. Everyone was appreciating the evening. The music was splendid, the guests resplendent in their finery, the food excellent, the Champagne superb, some of which Hale had insisted on providing, the moon full, in a clear December sky with stars. Divine.

A large group had just finished a dance and come to the buffet for refreshment and Elizabeth was seated on the other side of the group from the buffet awaiting Hale. Elizabeth caught Suzanne's eye and beckoned her over.

'How are you? I see you and Paulus are enjoying the evening,' Elizabeth said with life when Suzanne sat down beside her.

'Oh Elizabeth it is a lovely evening, truly lovely. Everything is beautifully arranged. And everyone is in fine spirits,' Suzanne replied, all appreciation.

'I'm so happy. And tell me how are you?', Elizabeth asked in a personal tone, leaning in toward Suzanne.

'I am very happy. Paulus and I are to be married next month in a small ceremony, only close family, in my home. I am happy and thankful. I had thought that I would remain alone, and not marry. And I was not unhappy, I was content. The prospect of sharing life now with Paulus is a most happy anticipation,' Suzanne said.

'Yes', Elizabeth said slowly. 'Sharing life, this is a different prospect. Tell me, what does that conjure, what does the horizon look like now?'

'Oh Elizabeth, the horizon is alive now, verdant, and bathed in bright sunlight', and she laughed at her artist's image. Elizabeth saw in Suzanne's eyes life she'd not seen there before, new life. Suzanne's expression had always been placid, content. Now her skin glowed and her face was alive, her expression more animated. She took Elizabeth's hand and held it saying, 'You have much to do with this. Thank you from the bottom of my heart.'

Hale was approaching with two small plates of dainties. Suzanne noticing him smiled and rose from her seat.

'Happy New Year Elizabeth', and she was gone into the crowd of party guests.

'Suzanne and Paulus look happy', Hale said to Elizabeth as he handed her the plate he had prepared for her.

Elizabeth thanked him and was silent for a few moments. Hale waited, aware of Elizabeth's interest in Suzanne and Paulus's new found happiness.

Then she said, 'What do you think of such a change? It is certainly very good to see Suzanne more alive, and Paulus more alive too, and most thankful for', she continued slowly, 'having let pride go', she stopped.

Hale, watching her expression said, 'Certainly it is good to see people happy', he paused. He could see Elizabeth reflecting, listening. 'Happiness is to be pursued. And one can only pursue it, being oneself', he stopped.

Elizabeth turned to him now, and slowly added, 'This is what I have been thinking about. How important it is to know oneself well. One wonders, having lived half one's life on one's own', she paused, 'there must be a good reason one has done so.'

After a few moments Hale said, 'Happiness doubled is very inviting. Perhaps, it is a question of time and timing. Only a certain amount of time, not all the time, sharing life. If one is able to well appreciate life on one's own, perhaps this is why one is able to well appreciate life shared with others, or another.' He looked at Elizabeth and she turned to him in response, but said nothing. He asked, 'Is the question, the right other? Is the ability to be happy on one's own an indication that one should remain so? Or, is it perhaps this very capacity that also enables one to share deeply, enjoy life fully with another?' He waited some minutes for her response.

And it was indirect when it came, 'Yes', she responded as though from far away and her accent on the word was as a question to herself.

'I've been wondering about pride, my pride', she offered.

'Yes', is all he said, and waited.

'The other day, for the first time since childhood, I got down on my knees to pray.'

'Yes', he said more softly.

'I felt it. I felt it, as I got down. And it was there as I continued to kneel and pray. I felt the pride that has subjected me to it and would have continued to subject me. Where as in making myself servant to that beyond myself, to God, pride could not subject me. And in having knelt, pride dissipated', she stopped.

A moment passed and Hale said, 'Yes', in understanding.

She had been looking out to the room and beyond quite unaware, unusually so, of her surroundings. His word brought her back and she turned to him. This time looking right into him, she smiled in thankfulness for his understanding.

Elizabeth put her hand on his forearm, and resting it there for a moment, looking at him, smiling, asked, 'Shall we dance?'

Hale rose and taking her arm fully in his led her to the dance floor. Her feet, lighter now, seemed to fly just above the wood floor. And their whirls seemed lighter and faster too. Then the orchestra changed to a slower waltz. Hale held her more closely. She simply moved and enjoyed moving to the music, unaware of anything else.

Hale whispered to her, 'Happy New Year Elizabeth.'

'Happy New Year Hale', Elizabeth replied.

As Hale moved them across the floor they were silent. Then he asked, 'Is that your friend Clarity dancing with Sir John Beresford?' he turned her about to see the pair.

'Yes, that is Clarity. So that is Sir John', Elizabeth's voice inquired into more than his identity.

'You don't know him then?', Hale responded, surprised.

'No. Lady Jane asked if I might include him as he has returned to London for Christmas and New Year', said Elizabeth.

'He has quite a reputation', Hale said.

'A reputation for what?', Elizabeth asked with a note of concern.

'For being an adventurer. He is not a rogue', Hale confirmed.

Elizabeth's concern evaporated, 'No . . . he could not be if Jane suggested him.'

'Does Jane know Clarity?', Hale inquired.

Elizabeth looked at him directly, 'She has met Clarity.'

'I wonder if Lady Jane is doing what Elizabeth has done?', Hale gave Elizabeth a full smile.

'Do you mean set things up for them?', Elizabeth sounded astonished.

'Don't be too surprised. She must have introduced them', Hale said with emphasis.

'Yes', Elizabeth replied softly.

Just then Hale whirled them about and over to where Clarity and Sir John were dancing.

Elizabeth, only somewhat surprised at Hale, eager to speak with her friend, said, 'Clarity how are you my dear?', as Hale moved in very close with Elizabeth should she wish to greet her friend with a kiss.

Sir John had instantly reciprocated the manoeuvre bringing Clarity closer to Elizabeth. The two exchanged a kiss on the cheek.

'Elizabeth I am so happy to be at Tudor Court and at your lovely ball,' Clarity enthused, reaching out with her free hand to squeeze Elizabeth's hand. 'May I introduce Sir John Beresford, Elizabeth Fennington.'

'Enchanted Elizabeth. Thank you for including me. May I congratulate you on a superb evening, a perfect New Year ball', said Sir John in a strong manly resonating voice.

'Thank you', Elizabeth replied observing him closely and noting the warmth of his charm.

'We have met before', Sir John addressed Hale. 'It is good to see you again and this evening Fenwick.'

'It is good to see you again. Take good care of Clarity. She is a dear friend of Elizabeth's', Hale injected a somewhat formal protective note as he smiled at Clarity.

'Duly noted', said Sir John. 'Lady Jane gave me the same injecture.'

'Sir John knows Roger Balerer and has been to Africa to see the work his foundation does', Clarity offered.

'That's right', Hale acknowledged. 'You are a financial supporter of Roger's foundation.'

Sir John gave a slight nod and smile and whisked Clarity off.

'He seems alright', said Elizabeth. 'In fact, I like him. I imagine that his somewhat casual countenance belies a far more serious nature and a good character', she finished.

'You are right. Our little encounter just now reminded me of who Beresford is', replied Hale.

Elizabeth gave Hale her full attention.

'He was knighted due directly to his courage in a dogfight over China. He is apparently a great and bold fighter pilot and was working for a time with the RAF on some undisclosed mission. They strayed into Chinese airspace and were attacked by no less than fifteen Chinese fighter jets. John and his three other RAF fighters took down five of their planes and the Chinese bugged out.'

'Do you mean he was the leader?', she asked.

'Oh yes. One of the things he is reputed to have is a genius for flying.'

'Something of a Renaissance man', Elizabeth conjectured.

'More, he is a classic', replied Hale. 'I think Clarity is in good hands.'

A group of seven old friends, making their way from the Great Room at 3:30 in the morning, had become fully engaged in a conversation that kept them pausing along the halls. Having stopped numerous times in the halls from the Great Room to the entrance of Tudor Court they slowly made their way toward the foyer. Elizabeth and Hale sat together in the parlour with the doors fully open waiting for Elizabeth's last guests to take their leave. Not wishing to make anyone feel that she was waiting Elizabeth let Chalmers manage their exit.

Chalmers stood at the entrance to the parlour and said, 'That is everyone Mamam. Goodnight and Happy New Year.'

'Thank you very much Chalmers. Goodnight. Happy New Year', Elizabeth smiled at her butler.

'Do you know I believe many guests must have left not long after midnight, and for the first time I did not say goodnight to them all', Elizabeth said to Hale at 4:00AM.

'I don't think they took it to mean anything other then perhaps you were enjoying yourself at New Year', he replied.

'Yes, of course you are right. And I have enjoyed myself', she paused with her lovely smile upon him. 'You've used that word 'perhaps' a number of times this evening', she continued.

'Perhaps I don't wish for my strong manner to have you retreat from me in any way', he smiled. Elizabeth laughed and he laughed with her.

'I have enjoyed the evening very much', she said. 'And I have appreciated very much indeed your understanding. I've never said very much of what is on my mind at a deeper level to anyone. My father often used to know what was on my mind and he would bring it up. He'd say a word or two. But I'd just listen. It was very good to be able to speak with you this evening.' She paused and then said, 'And the dancing was lovely. It was a very good New Year.'

He took her hands and leaning in kissed one cheek and then the other as he had done many times before but this time taking an extra moment. 'It was a very good New Year', he replied strongly.

'Goodnight', they said to each other in unison at the oak door.

CHAPTER THIRTEEN

PRIDE UNDONE REVISITED

Elizabeth and Clarity had a good lie in New Year's Day. When they did rise they met in the kitchen for toast and tea.

'A good walk, do you think?', Elizabeth asked simply.

'A good walk sounds perfect', replied her friend.

They were quiet for a time, only commenting on the freshness of the air, the hollyhock, and the blue sky. They walked from the garden out to the meadow toward the stream and the forest.

'Are you going to tell me about your evening?', Elizabeth asked.

'Yes, I spent most of the evening with Sir John. Will you tell me of yours? I noticed that you spent all the evening with Hale Fenwick', Clarity exclaimed.

Elizabeth laughing said, 'Yes I did. Hale arrived early, took me straight to the ballroom, ordered the orchestra to play the Viennese Waltz and that began an evening of dancing. It was very much what I was hoping for'. And Elizabeth laughed again.

'How wonderful', Clarity enthused as she took and squeezed her friend's hand.

'Tell me about John Beresford. What do you think of him?', Elizabeth spoke more seriously.

'I will', Clarity said and paused. There was a silence as Clarity thought and then began. 'I think he is a very serious man. One does not notice this at first. His seriousness, depth actually, reveals itself gradually, subtlety. I like his depth very much', Clarity stopped.

Elizabeth had been watching Clarity's face. Her serious expression revealed a deep thoughtfulness. Elizabeth waited.

Clarity continued, 'It was very good to learn that he has been where I am working. We spoke of that at length. He remembered a lot about the geography. He is very aware. He remembered the surrounding area, and he also remembered the people, and the children. A few of the children he met are still there. He remembered them, their names, and details about them that I would not remember if I was not with them everyday. He is quite insightful', she paused in reflection again. Then she added, 'He is unusual.'

They walked along the stream, not wading in this time, but enjoying the sound of the water as it continued to move ever onward to its destination.

'He asked about how I am in Africa. He immediately related to the kind of aloneness that arises from being far from the familiar, far from what is and can be home. He understood the fulfilment of being with the children who are so appreciative of care and love, so very responsive to love.'

Elizabeth was quiet, listening very closely to her friend.

'He is a very strong and unusual man', Clarity stopped speaking and stopped walking. Elizabeth stopped beside her.

'Yes, I agree. He is unusual', said Elizabeth.

Then Clarity said, 'I think I am in love with him Elizabeth.'

Elizabeth looked into the depths of her friend's eyes to see her more fully. Clarity said, 'It frightens me. I don't know how I could love someone so quickly.'

'He is a special man', Elizabeth said. 'It is perhaps because you are both special people. Hale told me something about him.'

'What did he say?', Clarity asked keenly.

'He said John was knighted due to great courage as the lead pilot in a dogfight over China.'

Clarity caught her breath.

'Did he tell you that story?', Elizabeth asked.

'No. I don't think he would', she answered simply.

'No', Elizabeth agreed.

'What should I do?', Clarity asked.

'What do you mean?', Elizabeth replied.

'What should I do about John?'

'What has he said to you?', Elizabeth inquired.

'He is coming to see me here in about an hour', Clarity said.

'Oh', was all Elizabeth could say.

'I think, no . . . I feel . . . that he is going to ask me to join him in Israel', Clarity said.

'What?', Elizabeth exclaimed.

'Yes, I think he is going to ask me to marry him', her friend said.

'Oh', Elizabeth replied again.

There was a long pause where neither spoke, though simultaneously they began to walk again.

After many minutes Clarity spoke, 'You spoke about understanding, someone understanding you. John understands. He understands so very much. And he understands me', she stopped walking. Elizabeth stopped beside her. 'If he does ask, I believe I will say yes.'

The sun was beaming down upon them, and it was warm, unusually so for a New Year's Day. The two friends turned to one another and warmly embraced.

Clarity and Elizabeth discussed what would be best, comfortable for Clarity and for John Beresford. They both agreed that the day was warm enough to be outdoors. Clarity wanted to be outdoors and Elizabeth thought that John would be in his element outdoors. Clarity agreed, appreciative of Elizabeth's awareness. Chalmers was instructed that when Sir John arrived he was to be led directly to the back garden.

'You like him too, don't you?', Clarity asked Elizabeth almost rhetorically.

'Yes. You know I do. Otherwise I would have said something to encourage you to wait', her friend replied.

'Yes I know', Clarity responded with an endearing smile.

'But you my dear must love him', Elizabeth said seriously.

'I do', Clarity responded without hesitation.

'Yes, I see that you do, and it is good that you know you love him', Elizabeth said. 'I will be in the library should you want me', Elizabeth ended softly.

'Of course we will want you', Clarity responded with energy. 'John will want your permission', she informed Elizabeth.

'Oh goodness, I hadn't thought of that', Elizabeth said.

'As my dearest friend, you are family really', Clarity added.

Elizabeth kissed Clarity's forehead, 'God bless you my dear.' And she left the garden for the library.

Chalmers guided Sir John to the back garden, directing him toward the other end. Clarity sat alone on a wooden bench beneath a towering Scots pine. Sir John paused beneath the enormous elm tree that stood high above the other trees and as at the entrance to the place where Clarity sat. They saw each other in the same moment. Sir John slowly smiled, intensely and comfortably focused upon Clarity. She responded with a slow smile, still, comfortable, happy. Sir John walked down to her from the mound where he had stood. Extending his arm he took her hand in his silently asking her to stand. She did and he led her over to an enormous hedgerow which was green in all seasons and open to the sky. He knelt.

'My dear Clarity, dear to me now, dear to me forever, may we join our lives this day in spirit and love and in a day shortly to come, under God? May we live together and share the time God gives us here and realise the life he wills us in eternity? Will you marry me?'

'Yes', she responded with a great warmth and a deep love.

A few days after New Year Hale Fenwick sounded the door knocker at Tudor Court. While he thought Elizabeth might be home he did not know. Late that morning he had clipped some holly and ivy from his bushes and brought the sprigs, a simple posy, for her.

'Good afternoon sir', Chalmers greeted him after opening the door.

'Good afternoon Chalmers. Is Miss Elizabeth at home?', Hale inquired.

'Yes sir she is. Shall I announce you?'

'Please. Thank you', Hale replied.

'Please come in sir', Chalmers stepped back. 'Make yourself comfortable. Miss Elizabeth is in the library. I will be just a few moments.'

Hale stood in the foyer of Tudor Court. He stood quietly, appreciating the entrance to Elizabeth's home, the high ceilings, the old wood, the simplicity of well considered design, the plentiful natural light, and the history that bestowed character. He could feel the sprig of holly between his fingers and smiled to himself. It too was simple, a representation of the season, the time of year, an offering from the garden. He knew he would like very much a good conversation and he had been thinking of Elizabeth, perhaps she would like one too. And in his mind this is why he had come. Elizabeth came gliding down the hallway, her figure highlighted by the sunlight behind her. Hale could see her hair move with the motion of her body.

'Hale, thank you for thinking of me', she smiled and stretched out her hands to her visitor as she was wont to do. He smiled and taking one hand, with the other proferred the posy. She smiled, and taking it in the fingers of her free hand twirled it, appreciating the green and the red that together accentuated each other. He squeezed the hand he held.

'Thank you for welcoming me', he replied.

They paused to learn the other's wish. And in seeing the same intention in the other's eyes, both laughed simultaneously.

'Come do. I've been sitting in the library thinking I would read, but I've been daydreaming instead', and she took his arm to lead him to the library and show him where she had just been.

Elizabeth moved naturally to her favourite seat near the south window and sat down. In an instant she realised she had assumed Hale's presence and not offered him a place.

'Oh, how rude, where would you like to sit?', she asked. But in the same instant Hale seated himself in a burgundy leather backed and firm seated wood framed chair, not immediately beside her, yet near.

He smiled, 'This is perfectly comfortable. It offers a good view of the room and is well placed if one wishes a good conversation', he said.

Elizabeth was looking at him, smiling, and realising she was pleased for his company in her library she responded, 'A good conversation, that sounds very good indeed.'

'Perhaps we can pick up on your musings at New Year, pride, sharing life, knowing oneself', he said.

'How is it that you understand?', she asked delighted. 'I think this is what I have been day dreaming about. I've been thinking about the fact of pride being present and unrecognised. And too, the idea of kneeling, finding a way to have pride dissipate to find a better way for one's life', Elizabeth responded.

After a moment Hale said, 'Years back a colleague came to me to talk. He was distraught about something. He was a well intentioned fellow, but he could not seem to get through a barrier he had. It was a generalised barrier he kept running up against as opposed to a particular situation that needed addressing. He had come to me I think simply to unburden himself. And so I listened. As I listened it appeared that there was something he did not, could not, see. I knew him as a man of faith. And as I listened the fact of his faith kept coming to mind. I realised that there was a conflict between the fact of his faith and his problem. If he truly believed why did he have this problem? Then it struck me, pride. And I asked the question which needed asking, 'Do you kneel when praying?' There was a very long silence that followed. He did not want to answer. He was ashamed. Finally he did answer, 'No.' I nodded. While we said nothing more about it, I could see by his expression that he knew now his problem was uncovered. Pride. And he knew that he had been offered a remedy', Hale finished.

'That's a good story', Elizabeth said quietly. 'I have done the kneeling and I'm doing it. I'm wondering what else there is. You see, I want to be the best, the finest really, of whom I've been given to be', she paused.

'Yes, I know', Hale said.

She looked directly at him,'You know?', she asked incredulous.

'Yes I know', he replied simply.

Her puzzled look made him smile but he said nothing. They sat for a couple of minutes, Elizabeth reflecting.

'Shall we go for a walk?', Elizabeth asked.

'Yes, I brought my boots, they're in the car. Shall I fetch them?'

'Do. And will you stay for a late lunch afterward?', she asked smiling warmly.

'I will'', he smiled back.

'Come straight through to the garden and we'll meet there. I'll run up and change', she said. They left the library together.

Hale brought his Wellingtons to Elizabeth's door with the most direct access to the garden. He put them on and waited for her in the garden. How lucky we are in England he thought, as he often had, for even in the winter there is green. The air is fresh from the rain, and particularly fresh in the garden. The bushes retain their foliage and the ground is soft, I can smell the earth. He strolled the immediate grounds. I wonder at the conversation we can have. The idea of pride, with some thinking, can lead to a very good conversation. Elizabeth is thinking about pride, life, why one shares life. Hale, absorbing the beauty of Tudor Court's garden thought of the faces he'd seen and the people he'd met at Tudor Court and of Elizabeth. Elizabeth shares her home and its beauty with neighbours, and many others who benefit from time here. What am I thinking? Observing Elizabeth has me recognise that I too must think about the way in which I should invest the rest of my life. He smiled to himself. Elizabeth has a way, a very special way, which discerns who people are. She discerns their character, and recognises something they need in order to better themselves. And somehow, and he laughed aloud, Tudor Court helps provide that.

'What are you laughing about?', Elizabeth spoke from the garden gate as she came through it.

'Hullo, I was enjoying your garden and thinking about you and Tudor Court', he said.

'Thank you. I'm hoping you will help', she said.

Hale raised a brow, seeking to learn Elizabeth's thinking from her face. She smiled at him and tipped her head to indicate they should go deeper into the garden. They did not speak for a couple of minutes.

Then Elizabeth continued, 'Help . . . yes. That is not an easy word to use. Yet, I'm thankful I can say it. I think it means I'm letting go of pride.'

Hale smiled, 'Yes, I think it does', he was listening.

'I'm thankful too for being able to speak to what is on my mind. Having someone who will listen and who can understand is a privilege.' They kept walking. The chirping of the birds was more frequent now.

Elizabeth continued, 'I've always thought, even as a child, in a romantic way about sharing life with a man, of being in love. And when I did think about love the colours of life were bright and full of sunshine and happy days. This does sound like a child's vision. In some way I still think similarly. Though now I understand more of life and think of love in a much deeper way. Do you know?', she asked rhetorically, 'No you probably don't know, I've had seven marriage proposals.'

Hale was walking behind her as they were ducking under low hanging branches. He smiled, confirming a general thought he had on the subject of Elizabeth and marriage. He said nothing and continued to listen.

Elizabeth continued sharing her thoughts, 'I've not really wanted to marry. I've quite enjoyed my independence.'

'Yes, that I can see', Hale said emphatically. Elizabeth turned around to see his face, and seeing his smile smiled too.

Then she said, 'There was a wonderful minister in New York and when I lived there I went to hear him every Sunday. He said we are smiled into smiling and loved into loving.'

Hale said slowly, 'Yes, I can see that.'

'Yet I think I might have married', Elizabeth was connecting thoughts in her mind.

'The right fellow, you mean?', Hale asked.

'Yes', she said. 'Were you ever married?', Elizabeth suddenly asked.

'Yes. When I was twenty two I married my third cousin once removed.'

'What? What does that mean?', she asked.

'I don't know exactly, distant, a rather distant cousin', he replied and continued. 'We'd known each other always, played together as children, grew up together.'

'That must have been very nice', Elizabeth commented, pondering.

'It was. And after all that growing together we grew apart', he laughed. 'We were only married for a year.'

'Were you sad? When it ended', she asked.

'Yes, though not as sad as I would have thought. You see I like my independence too', Hale said.

'It is very nice though to have someone one can really talk with', she said, her voice alight with gratefulness.

'Yes it is', he said firmly.

They had come through the bracken and now before them was the meadow backed with enormous and very old oak trees that stretching up to the sky bring heavenly beauty to earth.

'The stream is widest and flows quickest just into the trees on the other side of the meadow. Let's go there', Elizabeth said and started through the grass.

'It is beautiful here', he said. 'It is, I think, even more so than Fenwood.'

'Oh but Fenwood is ancient. You were there before the Tudors', she responded with fervour. And she began to run toward the trees where the stream flowed quickest. Hale ran too, quickly passing her. He looked back over his shoulder laughing. This made Elizabeth run faster, as he knew it would. They were laughing, and running, exhilarated. This made them laugh more deeply, a laughter echoing a childlike love of life.

As soon as they reached the stream they both waded in. Elizabeth had put on her Wellingtons too, perhaps instinctively for this moment. While the grasses were damp, she could have worn other boots for walking the meadow. For being in the stream the Wellingtons were best. They looked at one another, and after a moment, laughed again. Each recognising the feeling the other had at that moment. It was a childlike laughter of delight in anticipation of wading into a stream and the fun to be had, recognised, born of an ancient childhood ritual.

'The current pushes you a little doesn't it', Hale said rhetorically.

'You have to push back a bit', she replied in relay.

'I like the sound of the stream. It calls to one', Hale said. 'I wonder if this stream has the same source as mine?'

Elizabeth liked the sound of Hale's words. And thinking this a sweet thought said sweetly, 'Probably', and smiled at him.

They waded downstream.

'One needs people in one's life', Elizabeth said. 'But more, I think, one needs someone, one person who really loves you, and whom you love. A parent is usually this person', she was speaking more slowly than she usually did. Hale was listening.

'I'm an orphan, and have been for years now', she stopped. She felt herself tearing.

Hale waited and then said, 'My father is still alive. He is ninety two. He lives with his cousin or rather his cousin lives with him. My second cousin moved into one of the rooms in my father's house four years ago. He is eighty four and they both are still in pretty good shape. Actually they help each other.'

'That sounds sweet', Elizabeth responded.

'It is. You're right one needs someone with whom one is comfortable. In their case they've always known one another and gotten on well', he said.

'No one loves you like a parent', Elizabeth said more definitely.

'Yes, a parent has a particular love', Hale replied seriously. 'I can still go and see him. And when we can sit together in his den I feel his love. He has a great appreciation for the moment. When we are sitting there together, no one and nothing to disturb the moment, I feel his deep ability to draw on all the time we've shared, times I don't remember, probably even times when I was very small, times that have meaning for him. He brings all that together in the moment and I can feel his love and appreciation, there, in his presence.'

Tears came down Elizabeth's face for in the listening she felt the love of which Hale spoke. The cause of the tears was a touching of the depth in life that one can know but that does not arise in the daily routine. Something has to call it forth. It's door must be knocked upon and to knock one has to know the door is there. When the door is opened one must be vulnerable enough to enter.

'Oh I am happy for you that you have such moments with your father', Elizabeth's words were heartfelt.

'One is grateful', he said quietly.

Elizabeth said, 'I don't think I took the love my parents gave for granted. I loved them too and we had wonderful times together. And I had times too with each of them separately, vacations with my mom when Dad was working or travelling.

And when Mom died, Daddy and I would do things together, mostly time here or in Monaco. I miss my father's wisdom and Mom's sweet warmth', and the tears came again.

They had walked out of the stream and were walking the edge of the meadow. Hale, aware of Elizabeth's tears, was touched by her being able to let them come.

He said, 'It's hard to know the right answers. There is not one answer. One must find one's own way. Parents can guide but not lead. And one is very lucky indeed to find another who loves in the same way that one has been loved at home, when one has been truly loved.'

Elizabeth, listening, echoed his word, 'Home.'

He walked close beside her, just the right distance. Elizabeth was thankful to have him there. And she recognised that she was comfortable with Hale.

'Home', Elizabeth spoke the word again. 'That feeling of home signifies something very particular. Where does one feel at home? Some probably do not even feel at home, at home.' She paused.

Hale said, 'Yes, I have had too many friends over the years who did not feel at home in their house, with their family.'

Elizabeth looked at Hale directly and gave a slight shake of her head, and then said, 'If one can feel at home, other than in one's home, it speaks to the same kind of love that one found at home.' A slow smile came to Hale's face, and he nodded slowly.

Then he quoted, '"To be happy at home is the end of all labour", Samuel Johnson.'

Hale had always known his comfort with Elizabeth. He had sensed at the time of the dinner she had arranged for Suzanne and Paulus that Elizabeth was thinking about life, about what sharing life would mean. He now understood that it was this recognition that had moved him to come early at New Year. He knew Elizabeth loved to dance, and he enjoyed dancing. He knew dancing would be a lovely time. And now he was thankful to have this time to get to know Elizabeth.

Elizabeth said, 'I've never really needed anyone. I think most people need others, or one other. Years ago a boyfriend said, "You don't need anyone', and he left. It hurt at the time. I think because there was truth there. But I don't know that it is one hundred percent true', she let the thought hang in the air.

Hale nodded, and then said, 'I think I know what you mean.'

'Yes?', she wondered, waiting.

'I think, the same could be said of me. I don't truly need anyone. What might this mean for you and me?', he asked.

Elizabeth asked in return, 'You and me?'

'Could two people, neither of whom really needs another, share life?', he said directly.

She smiled, respecting his courage and forthrightness.

'I don't know', she answered honestly.

He said, ' . . . One would think . . . that where one person doesn't need another yet could enjoy, want, another, and that other did need someone it could be a good match. Most need to be needed but when neither needs another it is not a necessary match.'

Elizabeth stopped, looking out to the expanse of meadow, she said. 'How refreshing this is.' Her voice rang out, 'This air, being by the water, and you', she turned to Hale who stood a few feet away looking at her. 'Your openness encourages the same in me. It is refreshing.'

'Ah but you are open. Your nature is so', he replied.

'Yes, however you offer the opportunity for practise', she smiled.

'Well I'm glad of it', Hale said.

'Shall we walk round the edge of the trees to the other side?', Elizabeth asked.

'Yes', Hale replied with a smile.

'I'm wondering if there's something else you may think about', he paused a moment.

'Yes?', Elizabeth responded immediately.

'The end. Do you think about the end?', Hale asked.

Elizabeth did not respond immediately. They walked along the dirt path edging the forest and a number of moments passed.

Then she said seriously, 'Yes, I have done. I don't want to have any regrets. All my life as an adult I've wanted to be the best person I can be, character wise. Now there is something else. From here forward it is a deeper belief in God that I seek, a belief or relationship, which allows one to rest in him. It is important that I make my best effort. I believe life is to be no longer on my own with focus for my character. I feel a broader responsibility. My responsibility is to God', she stopped.

Hale considered Elizabeth's words. He realised that he had known this about Elizabeth. 'Yes, I've known this about you', he said.

Elizabeth considered his face. It touched her that someone would care about life so much that without any other motive one would pay this kind of attention. They continued to walk.

'I suppose I can say something similar', he said. 'There is a way of being, as you say closer to one's maker, and one walks that path. And when you do so for many years, perhaps not even always out of choice, you know very well, very clearly, when you step off the path. One's conscience pricks and steers you right back on.'

'That', Elizabeth responded, 'is a finely tuned conscience.'

He said. 'Well, I guess it is as you say, one wants to uphold oneself to a standard one can stomach.'

'And this does include the end, doesn't it?', Elizabeth said, asking him.

'Yes it does', Hale replied. 'One must consider the whole picture to have it become present with one. One can see that the days add to the whole picture and to the end.'

'It is a question for God. How may I best live my life? Teach me to number my days that I may know mine end', Elizabeth quoted.

'To live with the end in mind.', Hale responded.

She nodded. 'And what is one's responsibility to one's fellow man?', she asked herself and Hale.

'Love thy neighbour as thyself', he repeated. 'This is a hard one. Yet I believe you have done this and you do this. It is expressed in your invitation and your care with guests to Tudor Court. And what of your writing, and your reviews? Are you not encouraging others to be discerning, to consider the finest and not merely look to be entertained? I think you are. You've done a great good for Paulus', he finished.

Elizabeth, listening, finally said, 'There is something, I've been thinking about that Clarity understands.

'Clarity', Hale responded. 'Yes . . .', he encouraged her.

'Yes,', Elizabeth smiled. 'She understands life. It is a funny thing to say but I believe few do.'

'I believe that is true', Hale replied.

'Isn't it a shame?', Elizabeth continued. 'Each of us has been given life and we make choices about our life helping create the life we live, and should lead. But often one goes about it in a stumbly bumbly way and without the reflection needed to understand and lead it', she said.

Hale responded, 'Even if one has been given a good introduction, a solid upbringing with parents who care enough, who know to pay the attention right from the start, it takes something more. It takes a personal appreciation for the personal responsibility one has for the gift of life given. If the parent has this sense of appreciation the child has a distinct advantage. And an advantage that cannot be legislated.'

'Yes', Elizabeth was listening.

'Then the child too must develop independently, this love, this love of life, self, and the appreciation that deepens love and responsibility', Hale added.

'How is it that you came to understand?', Elizabeth asked.

Hale was thinking about his reply, 'I don't know. Perhaps a will to understand. Perhaps a need. Our parents loved us. That's always a good beginning. Yet people have vastly different capacities to love and sometimes the love a parent can give is not the kind the child needs. Perhaps better put, the child needs a love with something particular.'

Elizabeth asked gently, 'Was that your case?'

Slowly Hale replied, 'Yes I suppose it was. And this is where the need came in. A need to find that particular something that wasn't there.' They were quiet. Then Hale said, 'I think you were given exactly the love you needed', and he smiled at her.

Elizabeth said, 'Yes I believe I was.'

'And, you haven't aberrated that love', Hale added.

'What do you mean?', she asked.

'I mean, as Paulus had done. Whatever he was given, he added or kept 'pride'. And in doing so, in mixing in a great deal of pride he became an aberrant from what he was meant to be. As we can now see from the change that he has been able to make', Hale said.

Elizabeth nodded in understanding. 'It's kind of complicated', she said.

'It's probably very simple. It's when we complicate things that we get all mixed up', Hale said.

'Is it that we must be on our guard, to protect our fort, keep it intact? Is it that when we let our guard down that confusion sets in, we are weakened to worldly ways, like pride?', Elizabeth was asking herself as much as she was asking Hale.

'One must get clear what is most important. If one registers that there are less than a handful of things in life that are truly important, it is quite simple', he said.

Elizabeth smiled and asked, 'Do you think it is time for lunch?'

They entered at the back of the house leaving their boots at the door and their outerwear on chairs in the hall. Then Elizabeth asked, 'Where would you like to eat? There is a small table in the dining room we can have set for us', she posed as an idea.

'Could we make our own lunch and eat in the kitchen?', Hale asked.

'Oh, that sounds like fun. Yes let's do that', Elizabeth replied enthusiastically.

When they entered the kitchen the cook's helper was putting silverware away.

'Hello Cathy', Elizabeth greeted her.

'Hello Mamam', she replied, startled and surprised to see Elizabeth.

'We are going to prepare our own lunch', Elizabeth said happily, adding, 'and eat here'.

'Yes Mamam', and Cathy left the kitchen.

'May I explore? And see what we may find for our lunch?', Hale asked as he looked about the kitchen.

'Certainly', Elizabeth replied. And they both moved toward the fridges.

They found vegetable soup, cold chicken, and a lovely bean salad. In a cupboard Hale found homemade bread, still warm, butter and jams. Hale laid the table the staff used, while Elizabeth found a pot and heated up the soup. When all was ready they sat down opposite one another.

'Isn't this fun', Elizabeth exclaimed.

'I often do this myself. But it is fun doing it with you', Hale replied.

Elizabeth smiled. 'Good for you', she said thinking that this simple action showed a lovely down to earth quality in Hale.

'I haven't done this before. I like these plates', she said examining the plate in hand. 'Made in England', she announced.'I like the simple design, and white, always a good choice.'

'It's funny isn't it', Hale said in response to Elizabeth's discovery of what she had not known about her own kitchen. 'What else might be discovered under our own noses if we altered our habits?', he suggested.

Elizabeth nodded as she served Hale some soup. They sat, thoroughly enjoying their meal, contented.

Hale asked, 'Do you like to plan, or have a plan, for life?'

Elizabeth pondered for a moment, then, 'No, I guess I don't.' Then she said, 'I plan, as you know, my gatherings here. And I plan to have them throughout the year but for December. Other than that I don't plan. When I haven't seen people, friends, those whom I want to see, I travel to see them. But I cannot say it is a plan. I do not have, as you ask, a plan for my life. Do you?,' she asked Hale.

'There is a sort of plan. I cannot say that I'm ambitious. I find ambitious sorts are a type that plan. However, I have set out a couple of plans in my life. After my early marriage went to rack and ruin, I decided I'd better do something with my life. I got involved with British tennis. I think you know I've always loved tennis', Hale said. Elizabeth nodded.

'They got a little money, and I got to help establish some new programs for young players and along the way meet some of the really good players, British and others. Some of them have charities in which they are involved. And later I got involved in one of them, Roger Balerer's schools in Africa. It has been very rewarding over ten years now. The tennis association has been more than twenty years', he stopped.

'I'm glad for you', Elizabeth exclaimed. 'I've wondered why I haven't done more, or become involved in that way.'

'You have done your work in a unique way. Your gatherings here are very well suited to who you are. And as a result you have served many who have wanted to help themselves, and may not have been able to do it otherwise', Hale said firmly.

'Do you think Paulus and Suzanne will be happy for a lifetime?', she asked.

'That we cannot answer', he said.

'But, that would be nice to see', Elizabeth said rather quietly, 'otherwise my work, as you refer to it, would not be as valuable.'

'Oh I don't agree. Yes it would be satisfying for you, to see a happy marriage, two people going through the rest of their lives happy. However ten years, two years, of happiness is better than none', Hale confirmed.

Elizabeth, recognising the truth in his words, nodded silently.

They had finished their lunch.

Hale said, 'Come to my house tomorrow and we'll have lunch in my sunroom', and he got up, picked up the dishes, and went to the sink with them.

Elizabeth sat for a moment, watching his back, knowing she would go and join Hale tomorrow.

'Yes, thank you', she said.

CHAPTER FOURTEEN

INDEPENDENCE UNDERSTOOD

'I'm going to Hale Fenwick's for lunch. What do you think?', Elizabeth made the statement asking her maid Ellen. Elizabeth stood before her mirror as she dressed in a dark green wool pant suit.

'What do I think Mamam?', Ellen was somewhat taken aback, surprised by her mistress's question.

'Yes. It will be just Hale and myself at lunch', she clarified.

'Oh', Ellen replied even more surprised.

'Well?', Elizabeth looked in the mirror at Ellen, an as yet unseen smile coming to her face.

'Well, I think that is very nice Mamam', she said.

'Do you?', Elizabeth was enjoying herself, playing a little with Ellen.

'Yes I do Mamam', Ellen, managing to gain a better hold of herself, spoke firmly this time.

'Why?', Elizabeth continued to press Ellen, though letting up with her eyes, no longer looking at her maid as she fastened the buttons of her jacket.

'Mr Hale seems a very nice fellow. And he is very attentive to you', she stated.

'Why do you say that?', Elizabeth now looked again at her own reflection, seeking Ellen's.

'I heard Mamam, he danced with you all evening at New Year', she replied.

'Oh you did?', Elizabeth smiled at her. 'Yes we did dance all evening. I thoroughly enjoyed myself Ellen', she said, now turning to Ellen. 'How do I look?', she inquired.

'Very well Mamam', Ellen replied.

'I will see you later', Elizabeth said as she took Ellen's hand briefly in her's, and taking up her hand bag, left the room.

When Elizabeth arrived at Fenwood she was led to the kitchen. There Hale had prepared a lunch for them and had placed it all in a picnic basket. He immediately took up the basket, took her arm, and said, 'May I escort you to our picnic?'

She laughed, 'Please do.'

Hale led her out of the kitchen, down the wide hallway and to the sunroom.

'Please be seated Miss Fennington', Hale spoke formally, with a broad smile as he gestured her to sit on a lovely two seater wood backed bench which appeared to be from another era, in a comfortable nook of the sunroom. The sunroom was filled with plants including a few trees and the light coming in through full length windows filled the room.

'What a beautiful space', Elizabeth exclaimed. 'It is charming. Why the ceiling must be fifteen feet up.'

'Eighteen', Hale replied. 'My mother decorated the sunroom. The statues, sculptures, paintings, plants, even the plant pots she choose with care', he said.

'Oh I can tell. What an eye she had for colour and what exquisite taste.'

Hale smiled, appreciating both Elizabeth's affinity with his mother's taste and the value she placed on the care his mother had taken for the space in which the two of them were about to enjoy their picnic. He spread a small cotton table cloth with a pastel flower pattern on the small wood table between them and now was placing the dishes and food.

'This thick cotton fabric is of an old design', Elizabeth said as she ran the palm of her hand along the fabric of the bench.

'You are right. I believe my mother purchased all that was left from a Milanese merchant's shoppe years ago. It is a rustic cotton the Italians like to use in their country villas. She had some woven into a settee for my parents bedroom.' Elizabeth smiled at him and paused.

'You've gone to some work here', Elizabeth said as she surveyed the place settings.

'It took me close to an hour to find the plates and silverware, glasses and the butter dish. I think the servants must be laughing now that I've sent them off.'

This time the bread was hot as Hale had asked the cook to bake it in good time for Elizabeth's arrival. And each of the three courses were accompanied by lots of hot bread and butter.

'My fingers are dripping with butter', Elizabeth exclaimed, enjoying herself.

'Me too. There's nothing quite like good hot homemade bread slathered with fresh country butter', Hale responded.

When they'd eaten they sat enjoying the space they'd made their own.

'I'm enjoying your company Elizabeth', Hale said.

'And I am enjoying yours,' and in another moment she said, 'I'm enjoying our time together.'

He waited for her.

'And given who we are, our natures, I'm thinking we may want to keep it like this', she paused to watch his response. He was listening.

'If we continue as we've begun we will have the chance of getting to know one another. This will be a privilege', she stopped.

Hale was looking at her, listening closely. For a moment he looked disappointed but then his expression changed. A smile came back to his face. He said, 'You know, I think you are right. Perhaps I was hoping we might be together, a couple', he said slowly. 'Yet, I think you are right. We could get to know one another better', he paused, 'this way.' His eyes rested upon her, and as they looked into one another they saw something. There was something that had always been there within each of them. Now it could arise, come forth, and be alive. Tears welled up in Elizabeth's eyes in gratefulness for Hale's understanding and in joy of life. Hale rose from his chair and taking Elizabeth's hand in his beckoned her to join him. 'Let's go outdoors for a few minutes', as he said this he picked up a sweater from a corner chair and draped it over her shoulders. They stepped outside.

'Let's do a circuit of the house', Hale said.

Fenwood Park is a much larger house than Tudor Court and their circuit took many minutes as they meandered amongst the old beech and great oaks that surrounded the house. The air was fresh and the sun, coming in and out of the grey and white clouds helped warm them. She smiled at him as they strolled near the house. Birds chirped in a nearby tree.

'I love the quiet of our countryside', Elizabeth said.

'I love it too', he replied.

She said, 'When I recognised a few years ago only a short time after my father died, that it was his understanding me that meant so much, I felt more alone without him. His love, a great deal of love I believe it takes to understand another person, was full and made no need for love of another kind. Your understanding makes me feel no longer alone', Elizabeth said.

'I wish I had known your father', Hale said in response to the first of what she had said. 'That you now feel no longer alone makes me happy', he said responding to what she had just spoken.

When they completed their circuit Hale and Elizabeth returned to the sunroom. She sat nestled in the love seat and he sat across in the chair where they'd shared lunch together. It was their own space and neither one spoke for some minutes.

Hale had been watching Elizabeth's face. Slowly a beautiful calm had come to her expression and when it was complete he said, 'I believe it is the way you and I are made, it is our nature that has us happy within ourselves, with God. And yet he would have each as happy as he or she can be. And so it is to be discovered how this may be.'

Hale's appreciation made her smile, and say, 'Yes. I see this more clearly now. He helps us doesn't he? When we are ready, when we are open for it, he shows us, he brings us to that which will help, to one who helps us see ourselves and understand life better.' She said her words very quietly, looking up at Hale. 'It is precious to know there is another who understands, cares, with whom one can relate', her voice was full of love.

'Your words are good to hear', Hale said slowly.

'Will you show me your home?', she asked. 'But not today. This place we have right here and now is perfect. I don't want to move.'

Hale laughed, 'Yes I'll show you my home as you ask. But you have seen every room, or almost.'

'Ah but this will be quite different. You weren't showing me.'

Hale laughed more fully, 'Alright. I look forward to it.'

Elizabeth relaxed into the back of the love seat and cozied up into one of its arms. 'I think I would have liked to have known your mother. She had a sense of beauty, an understanding for beauty', Elizabeth said.

Hale, appreciating Elizabeth's awareness, said, 'We are enjoying this sunroom now as we are because of her understanding.'

'Yes, and even the plants are delighting, they are thriving,' Elizabeth said. Suddenly she burst out with, 'Hale you must have a dog.' There was a pause.

Replying he said, 'Yes', with a question in his voice.

'Well, let's get you one', Elizabeth said sitting up.

'Do you mean right now?', he responded taking in her meaning.

'Yes', she said rising from the love seat.

Hale stood in response but said, 'Why the rush?'

'It's not a rush, it's the right thing', she replied.

'What kind of dog do you have in mind for me Miss Fennington?'

'I think you need a big dog. One who can keep up with you', she laughed. He laughed too.

'There is a breeder about twenty miles down the road. Let's try him first', she was walking to the door. And Hale was following her.

In the car Hale said as he turned into the road, 'I think you are crazy Miss Fennington.'

'Perhaps it is that I am spontaneous', and she gave him a sideways look and smile.

Hale said, 'You know, I love dogs. We had dogs growing up. I don't know why I haven't got one. I think this breeder has Wolfhounds, Irish Setters, and large Griffon's.'

'We'll see', Elizabeth replied.

As they drew up into the yard two Irish Wolfhounds stood observing them from the owner's kennel grounds. Hale said, 'Sure enough he has Irish Wolfhounds.'

'Oh aren't they lovely puppies', Elizabeth exclaimed, as she saw the kennels.

'Puppies! Oh I don't know about a puppy', Hale sounded startled, hesitating after he closed the car door. He stopped and stared at the large open kennels with puppies.

Elizabeth had skipped round to his side of the car, 'Of course you want a puppy. You want to bring him up to be fully your dog', she responded firmly and taking his arm, strode over to the kennel with all the Irish Wolfhound puppies. Hale, looking about for another kennel with full grown Wolfhounds, not seeing one reluctantly followed.

'Oh look at all the baby Wolfhounds', Elizabeth squealed.

Hale laughed as he stood beside her, absorbing her childlike excitement and enthusiasm.

'You have to wait to see *your* dog', she advised him as she knelt down in front of the large kennel cage to be closer to the puppies.

The puppies squeezed forward to be closer to her.

'Now kneel down here with me and look for your dog', Elizabeth directed him.

Hale knelt down obediently and he was about to ask what she meant, when another surge of puppies came forward toward him. Elizabeth looked sideways at him. A big smile filled Hale's face as he watched a dozen or more Wolfhound puppies push toward him. One dark grey puppy had just come out from the interior part of the kennel to see what all the commotion was. Elizabeth noticed him. In a moment she realised it was Hale he wanted for he immediately angled himself left toward Hale. As he pushed his way through fifteen or more puppies, he began to whimper. Hale noticed him. The little guy kept pushing his little body and squeezing through the other puppies to get to Hale. Elizabeth and Hale were silent watching him. Hale was now giving attention only to this puppy. He extended his hand to the fence. This made the puppy find his strength and he burst forward pushing the five dogs nearest him aside. As he reached Hale's hand his cold wet nose touched Hale's fingers and he barked for joy. Elizabeth and Hale knew this was the one.

'Oh what a good bark you have for such a little tyke', Elizabeth exclaimed to the little guy.

'Hello little one', Hale's voice was low and slow, and warm with endearment.

At the sound of Hale's voice the puppy gave a cross between a bark and a whimper asking it seemed for Hale to be his master.

Elizabeth was having a friendly chat with the kennel owner, the kennel keeper had gone into the kennel and retrieved the dark grey puppy for Hale. Hale was playing with the puppy he'd chosen and who had chosen Hale. The puppy was five weeks old, a little young to leave his mother. Elizabeth was assuring the owner that Hale would take the best care of him, nursing him as his own. She knew that the puppy would be all the closer to Hale if the owner would let him go now and the two would form the strongest of bonds. She explained that this is what she had experienced as a young girl when their neighbour had brought over a little five week old puppy for her. Finally the kennel owner agreed if Hale would come back in three days.

'You are going to have a lovely dog. I can tell Hale', Elizabeth said as they drove away.

'How can you tell?', he asked.

'Oh I just know. Don't you?', she responded with energy.

'Yes I think I do', he laughed. 'Thank you for insisting we go.'

'Did I insist?', she queried.

'Yes. You were definite that we were going to the kennel and that I was to get a dog. However, insist may not be quite right as you are ever charming. You are always charming Elizabeth', Hale said looking at her sideways.

Elizabeth said slowly, 'I'm not sure charm is so important.'

'It is not', Hale replied.'It can however be very welcome.'

'I suppose it helps things along. As for example the icing on a cake is a bonus to taste', she offered.

'That's it', he said with an upward lilt in his voice.

Elizabeth said contemplatively, 'I have thought of charm as an often superficial means to one getting along or of getting more of what one wants.'

'Charm is often used that way. One sees it at parties when someone who doesn't really want to be there but hasn't anything better to do, comes out and puts on the charm as party clothes', Hale offered.

'You're right. I have seen that', Elizabeth replied. 'How many people do that?', she asked, wondering.

'Too many', he said immediately.

'Now that I think about it I've seen it at my own parties', Elizabeth added.

Hale said nothing.

Then Elizabeth said, 'I've seen some spend the entire evening charming someone and for an end in mind.'

Hale nodded.

'Yes, sometimes I have seen guests talking, just talking, trying to be charming, to be part of the group, to fit in. To feel, I guess, accepted by what some must consider the right crowd', Elizabeth said.

'Yes', Hale said solemnly.

'Why? What kind of choice is this?', she asked herself aloud, thinking. 'Wouldn't one rather choose for oneself what is important? In other words, consider one's time and life important? Then one truly has something, oneself, to share with another', Elizabeth said with energy.

'Yes. However most do not have the security you possess', Hale replied.

'Do you think? Many of my guests have more wealth, position, influence, power, than do I', she responded.

'But not the true confidence you have. Your sense of wholeness, of being comfortable in your own skin, they do not have', Hale said. 'And it is this confidence which is required to be oneself.'

Elizabeth was quiet for a few moments. Then she said, 'You are right. They do not have that. And I am sorry that they do not. Can they obtain it?', she asked openly.

'I don't know', Hale said. 'Do you think Paulus has some of this feeling now, a greater sense of confidence in his own character?'

'He might, yes', she said. 'Confidence in his own character', she repeated Hale's words.

Hale said, 'I think that is what it is. A confidence in who one is. In contrast is the confidence built from externals, time, experience, successes, which is a contingent confidence. One cannot live from the place you live without the genuine article. And you have it.'

Elizabeth turned to him, looking at him, seeing him. She was seeing more of who Hale is.

'You know, I wonder sometimes why I give all the parties I do at Tudor Court', she said, and waited.

'One reason is you enjoy them', Hale moved into the silence.

'Yes', Elizabeth replied and waited.

Hale said, 'Another reason is likely that you instinctively know you are good for others. That is, that others, being at Tudor Court and in your presence are helped by being at your gatherings. They are better guided because your uncommon understanding and perspective are enlightening and your energy is enlivening. And in your understanding is not only a sense of energy there is the sense of what life means, what life should be, to be alive to it.'

Elizabeth listened, silent. Then she said, 'I suppose so.'

'You know so', Hale said emphatically, laughing.

Elizabeth laughed too, at herself.

'You see, you can laugh at yourself. A sure sign that you like yourself. In fact, I think you're crazy about yourself. You think you are the best darnedest thing to come along since the cart and horse!', Hale spoke through his laughter.

'Oh Hale that's a terrible thing to say', she clenched her fist and gave him a punch on his arm.

He laughed even more. They'd arrived and Hale stopped the car on his pebbled drive. He sprang out of the car and around to Elizabeth's side just as she was getting out. Hale whipped her up and over his shoulder before she knew what was happening and began to run around the drive with her. He was still laughing.

'Hale, what are you doing?', she shouted. 'Put me down.'

'Not yet', he said.

'You clown. Put me down', Elizabeth demanded.

'I will if you will have dinner with me tonight.'

'Oh, you're crazy', she replied.

'No. No. It is you who is crazy. Remember?'

'Ohh', and this time Elizabeth began pounding her fists on his back.

'Stop that pounding', he said matter of factly. 'It won't do you any good. Will you have dinner with me?'

'Yes. Yes, alright', she gave in.

He put her down and they faced one another on the drive. Hale was smiling broadly, Elizabeth suppressed a smile.

'Why do you want to have dinner with me?', she asked.

'Because you are so much fun to tease', and he gave a hearty laugh. 'Come on I'll take you home. Is your cook at home this evening?', he asked her in the car.

'Yes', Elizabeth answered.

'Alright, I won't have to bring anything', he smiled. Elizabeth just looked at him. And they were quiet for a time.

'I'll come at seven thirty', he said as he drove onto Elizabeth's drive.

That evening they dined at one end of the long table in Elizabeth's dining room. They had not spoken directly about where they would eat nor what they would wear. However both had dressed for dinner. Elizabeth wore a long mid-grey dress splashed with an attractive burgundy pattern. Hale wore a navy suit and a white shirt with a green and blue stripe.

Mary prepared roasted duck with a variety of vegetables all of which were laid out as buffet that they could serve themselves.

'Do I think too much of myself Hale?', Elizabeth asked.

'I don't believe you do. I believe you are justified', he said in earnest.

'It is important to me that my walk is a good and true walk ever closer to my maker,' she said even more earnestly.

'I know', he replied. 'It is part of your charm that you want to think very well of yourself, and can.'

'Ah but we said charm is often not a good thing', Elizabeth responded.

'We said charm is a pleasant thing if it is not used for an end. And, I think you believe that everyone should think very well of himself.'

'Yes, yes I do', she said strongly. 'I also think everyone should work on character.'

'Yes, and you are right. And in not doing so you believe they are wrong. Is that so?', he asked.

'Yes I do. I believe it is our personal responsibility to work on character.'

'I thought so', he said.

'You don't?', she was surprised he had not agreed with her.

'You said personal responsibility, that it is one's personal responsibility to work on his or her character. And I agree it is. However it is therefore also one's choice as to whether one does. And while I know you would not seek to interfere with that choice, you may wish to remember it is one's choice. And therefore that one should be tolerant and accept the person where they are when they do not meet your standard', he finished. There was a pause.

'Perhaps', she finally said. Then Elizabeth added, 'You see, we, each of us, has a personal responsibility to God. And this is true whether we recognise it or not. One's character is who one is, is who one has been given to be by God. We should tend it well. This is our sacred trust with God. What can be more important?', Elizabeth finished. Hale smiled at her.

'When is the next Tudor Court gathering?', Hale asked.

'I haven't thought about that', Elizabeth said.

'Why is that?', Hale asked.

'I don't know, except that you have been taking up my time', she smiled at him.

'I don't want to stop you', he left the rest hanging in the air.

'I don't know. I've been wondering if my guests' good purpose here is complete. Perhaps the main purpose of Tudor Court gatherings has been fulfilled', Elizabeth said.

Hale smiled and nodded. And looking at her with love said, 'Perhaps it has.'

He came around to the other side of the table where Elizabeth sat. He stood beside her. Elizabeth rose. He stepped back with her from the table and wrapped his left arm around her waist and holding her back with his right hand pulled her to him. He kissed her firmly on her mouth and held her for a long moment. Each felt the movement within as of rising to the heavens as each gave themselves in their kiss. As Elizabeth thought of it later this feeling is from where the phrase seventh heaven comes, two souls at home together.

'Will you be dining alone sir?', Nesmith asked his master.

'Yes Nesmith. Please tell Joseph, just something simple', Hale replied to his housekeeper.

Hale walked to his study. I should sit and think, he said to himself. He knew now he loved Elizabeth. He probably had loved her for years and never acknowledged it. 'I wonder', he spoke in an audible voice, as he sat in his dark brown leather wing chair facing the large window that looked out onto the south field. Did I push away my feelings? Deny them? I don't think so. It was more of a gradual process that has brought me to this point. It was an initial awakening to who she is, an awakening that grew to a realisation. When was that awakening? He tried to recall when he had first met Elizabeth. He could not remember. He did remember though his first time at Tudor

Court. I remember standing in the entrance way. I was with a few others, I don't recall whom. We had been invited to a party there. And what I remember is standing in the entry foyer taking in the ambience. The simple beauty of the house's design struck me. The architect, Henry Swithmore, was one with the ancients. Swithmore had true classic sensibility, his understanding and appreciation of the Greek and Roman style translated to the British was insuperable. The entrance was welcoming, warm, timeless. I recall now feeling strangely at home and I remember thinking how odd this felt as I have never felt at home anywhere but in my own home. Could Elizabeth feel at home at Fenwood? Could I give up Fenwood? Then he thought of Isabelle, his niece, she would love to live at Fenwood. I could give it her in trust. And I could visit. That is a possibility.

But that is getting ahead of things. Yes it is a feeling that has grown with time. It feels timeless, like I have always loved her. 'Before the Tudors', she had said. Yes, the Fenwood estate had been originally owned by his ancestor, John Fenwick, of the line of Henry II. Plantagenets. The Tudors came later. Elizabeth feels understood with me as she had been with her father. This makes me feel very good, deep inside. Does she know that I feel understood by her? She is right, a lot of love is required for understanding. The way to love someone in the way they need to be loved is to understand who the person is, and that requires standing back. Standing back is very hard when you love someone. That capacity to love, to understand first who someone is, is of a greater capacity than most possess. Yes, he thought to himself, people have vastly different capacities to love. There was a knock at his study door.

'Yes', he called.

The door opened, it was Nesmith his housekeeper.

'Sir, your dinner is ready. Did you want to eat in the dining room or shall I bring your dinner here for you?'

'Thank you Nesmith. Bring it here please', Hale replied.

He liked to be able to sit and think, without interruption. Nesmith would knock gently one more time. He could sit here all night thinking, waiting for his thoughts to arrive. He didn't need to do this as he knew what he thought. More, it was that he enjoyed thinking, connecting the dots, puzzling over important things. And then the dawning of understanding would come. That was the great thing. More, or even sometimes, new, understanding would come. There is nothing quite so sweet.

How blessed to feel understood in this world. Elizabeth had understood immediately when they had had that conversation on the walk by the stream at Tudor Court. He had not been loved the way he needed to be loved. His parents had not understood him. To find someone who understands you, who cares enough to stand back and see you for who you are, that is a great blessing. Just to know that there is someone in this world who understands you is a rare and precious thing. And here Elizabeth was, and on the same side of the stream. Hale laughed. He felt warm inside. Would she live here at Fenwood? It was a much larger estate, more than three thousand acres. She appreciates time, the timelessness of that which is classic. I'll have to ask her.

Nesmith had come quietly and entered with his dinner. He saw it there on the small circular wood table not far from where he sat. He hadn't noticed until this moment. What a good man. Nesmith understands. He smiled again. At least he understands that I like to reflect.

To have love in one's life, this made all the difference. Even if we do not become a couple, we are getting to know one another ever better. She could stay at Tudor Court and I at Fenwood. And that is not very far apart. We'd be pretty lucky. Elizabeth has been loved as she needed to be. Understood. Perhaps the two things meant the same thing. Yes, it takes a lot of love to understand someone, to stand back and see them. And then the understanding enables the kind of love needed by the other. I would have liked to have known Elizabeth's parents. Her father understood her. I would have liked to have known him.

He drew the salad, cold meats, and the homemade bread he loved toward him. Will she marry me? I really don't know. Does she love me? I certainly do not know. He laughed. As he ate he contemplated Elizabeth. And a smile, slow, firm, and full came to and stayed upon his face.

Elizabeth Fennington had one more gathering at Tudor Court. The guests included; Angus Erhly, Evangeline Ehrstwyle, Greg Edgar, Leticia Ulster, Paulus Pedigree and Suzanne Abbington French, the Weatherby's, Lady Jane Samuel, Esther Whyte, Sir Hamilton Atwater, Astrid Markum, Dame Catherine Wentworth, Elliot Newman, Syril Arlington, Alison Martin, Herbert Gainsberg, Edwin Barth, Joana Lester, Sir Joshua Tilling, Jack Blenheim, Wyatt Onwell, Elizabeth's neighbour Emmett Blumun and of course Bartholomew Atwater and Clarity Freeman and Sir John Beresford.

And Hale was there. He stood beside Elizabeth to greet the guests while Chalmers took their wraps and hats. They seemed to know that this was to be the last of the Tudor Court gatherings. And in some cases, the last time they would see the inside of Tudor Court, the last time they would be at Tudor Court.

If you had been watching you would have seen Evangeline Ehrstwhyle standing at the entrance to the Great Room breathing in the atmosphere. Leticia Ulster was peering into the library wondering at all the books, with a determined expression. For she was determined to go home and take a good survey of her own book shelves and purchase what was lacking in terms of the classics. Greg Edgar had a chance to redeem himself in the eyes of Wyatt Onwell. Angus Erhly, no longer angry, was happy to see Elizabeth happy and that so many good people graced Tudor Court. Paulus and Suzanne had sold their properties and had managed to purchase another old property which together they were making their home. And everyone was enjoying the openness and love of life expressed in Clarity Freeman. Clarity and Sir John were having a May wedding. When Clarity had called Elizabeth to tell her of the wedding she had asked if she would be bringing anyone. Elizabeth had answered with one word, Hale.

The last organised gathering at Tudor Court was a special evening, touched by the fresh beauty of early Spring, and blessed by the scent of new flowers and evening birdsong. Hale stood beside Elizabeth as they wished the Tudor Court guests, goodnight.

'Let us then implant this wisdom and let us exercise therein, that he may know the meaning of human desires, wealth, reputation, power, and may disdain these and strive after the highest.'

John Chrysostom
c. 345 – 407 A.D.

Made in the USA
Middletown, DE
29 January 2023

23239809R00135